Cedar Hollow Summer

A Demeter Society Story
BOOK 4

Books in the Demeter Society Series
by Amanda Schwantes
Enjoy as a series or read as stand-alones

Cedar Hollow Farm: Book 1
The Midwest Farmer's Guide to Love: Book 2
Christmas at Cherry Bounce Inn: Book 3
Cedar Hollow Summer: Book 4

Chapter One

In Which Earplugs Would've Come in Handy

Wesley Jacquemart: rural sex therapist and mobile librarian.

Had it really come to this?

Wes's career with the Door County Bookmobile had started out innocently enough.

Tom, one of the village's retired farmers, had stopped in one day in late fall. He stepped inside and wandered along the shelves of books on both sides of the bus. He tipped a few titles to read their covers before replacing them.

He sat down. He sighed.

If that had happened today, when Wes had ample experience with what the sit and sigh predicted, Wes would've hopped out for a moment, claiming an urgent need to check the tire pressure or have a look under the hood of his burgundy 1950s era mobile library. But that was a simpler time, a time when the unsuspecting Wes sat down alongside the elderly farmer and asked, "How's it going?"

"Oh well, you know how it is. Yup. Just hangin' in there."

"Is everything alright?" *Why? Why had Wes shown even a speck of curiosity?*

Tipping his battered John Deer baseball cap, Tom reached beneath it and scratched his balding head. "The wife is saying I snore."

Wes had nodded sympathetically. "Keeping her up at night?"

"Well, that's what she claims, but I'm not so sure." Tom pursed his lips and scowled. "She's taken to sleeping in the guest room. I told her she could wake me up if I started sawing logs, but she said that, if she has to wake me up, then she's awake too, and she has trouble getting back to sleep."

Wes could see her point there but, judging from the glower on Tom's face, it didn't appear that he would appreciate anyone else sharing his wife's view of things. Instead, Wes said, "There could be an upside. You're probably not accustomed to having that much space in bed."

"Yup. That was what I thought at first, too. It was kinda roomy, and when I asked around at Emma's Café I found out that a bunch of the guys have the same arrangement with their own better halves. But the unfortunate downside of the arrangement dawned on me pretty quick." Tom gave Wes a meaningful look.

Yes. The downside was obvious to Wes as well, who had recently reunited with his childhood sweetheart. "That sounds like quite a conundrum you've got there." Wes's impulse to sneak out and check the tires was born that very moment.

"Sure is. We haven't been...well, you know... as much as we used to when we were younger. And it's not just..." Tom made a twirling motion with his hand, "well, I miss the cuddling too. We keep the house cool at night, and winter will be here before we know it. I can't ask the guys what they do about *that* side of things."

Apparently he could ask Wes, though.

Wes was cornered in his own mobile library with no easy exit. This was a completely one of a kind experience for him. Nowhere else could a seventy-year-old man stroll into Wes's stationary vehicle and unburden himself so readily.

Perhaps this was something like the experience of being a taxi driver. The important difference here was that taxi passengers were usually strangers whose journeys lasted a finite amount of time. In Wes's case, the village was tiny, he ran into these people everywhere he went, and he was stuck in that parking lot until his scheduled departure at six o'clock.

"So, as I was saying," Tom interrupted his thoughts. "I'm stuck between a rock and a hard...well, you know." Tom looked to Wes as if waiting for him to present a brilliant solution for his marital difficulties.

Wes looked back as if pleading with Tom to run out the door without another word spoken about his hardships.

Wes opted for the cop-out. "I'm not a married man myself, so I'm not sure what to tell you. Maybe I snore too."

Tom scoffed at the notion. "Young guys like

you don't snore. Besides, you can't fool me. I saw Bea sneaking across the field from your cabin to her farm early one morning not a week ago."

So much for having any secrets in this town. "You've got me there." Wes suddenly became preoccupied with the returns drop box while pondering what precise shade of vermillion pulsed into every fold of his ears. Hey, there was an idea. "Maybe your wife could use earplugs?"

Tom pressed his lips together so tightly they disappeared. "How well do you think that'll go over?"

"I don't know. It might be alright. Maybe your wife misses..." Now it was Wes's turn to search for a word that wouldn't cause his face to turn red as well..."cuddling."

Standing up, chuckling, and patting Wes on the shoulder, Tom said, "You were right the first time. You're not married yet. Just you wait." He stood up, grabbed a book at random, and checked out. Tom left with *The Twenty-Something's Epic Guide to Adulting* tucked beneath his wiry plaid clad arm.

Wes had never been so sorry that his advice turned out to be helpful.

With marital harmony restored at his house that very evening, Tom advertised Wes's romantic wisdom far and wide from his perch on the red bench outside the front door of Emma's Cafe.

Soon what felt like the whole village was stopping by for advice, and Wes learned to spot those who were coming to him for a little chat from a mile away. They were the ones who aimlessly glanced at the books, just as Tom had, while other patrons came and went with their books and videos. The loiterers would stay for an hour or more sometimes, waiting for everyone else to clear out so that they could get some quality one-on-one time with their resident librarian slash personal life coach.

At this point, Wes knew everything he'd never wanted to know about these people: their sex lives (of course), but also their feuds, thwarted ambitions, secret crushes, and guilty consciences. It had been a year of learning, in no uncertain terms, that there are some things you can't un-hear. Would anyone be offended if Wes took his own advice and went the earplugs route? Probably, but desperate times called for desperate measures.

Who knew there was so much disquietude lurking beneath all these stoic Midwestern exteriors?

Seven months had passed since Tom's fateful visit, and the stream of those seeking Wes's sage wisdom and listening ear hadn't abated in the slightest. If anything, as the news of his successes grew, Wes's popularity blossomed as well.

On a lovely afternoon in late May, Wes pulled into the parking lot of Saint Mary of the Snows once more. He scanned the perimeter. There wasn't a patron in sight. The church parking lot was shared by Ed's Tavern, a practical necessity that was common around those parts thanks to churchgoers who wanted to be able to visit the pub after a long and fortifying mass.

A portly man in a too-small gray t-shirt stumbled out of the bar. Was he heading for the bookmobile? It wasn't uncommon for a day drinker to stop in for a chat. Those visits could get colorful to say the least. The man turned the other way, heading for the truck of a friend who'd arrived to pick him up.

"Hey there."

Wes whipped around to see Betsy climbing into the back of the bus. "Sorry," she said, "I didn't mean to startle you." Her wavy blonde hair spilled over her shoulders, mostly obscuring the thick straps of a form-fitting black dress. Her belly strained against its stretchy fabric. A silver bangle encircled her wrist. The only sign of possible strain were the worry lines that had recently formed in the corners of each of her bright blue eyes.

Wes smiled. He was in the clear. Betsy, despite the obvious complications in her life, wasn't one to overshare. "No worries. I just got here. Are you looking for something in particular?"

Betsy made a soft humming sound. Was that a yes or a no? She tipped the books, tilting her head to examine their titles. Why was she doing that? Was this what Wes thought it was? There was still time to jump ship and claim he needed to run inside the church to talk to Father Tim.

Wait.

Was he really going to run away from people now? This was getting silly. She was probably browsing.

Betsy sat down. She sighed.

"Wes?" she said.

"Yes…" He hadn't gotten out of the driver's seat yet. He gripped the door handle. It was now or never.

"Can I talk to you about something?"

Now it was Wes's turn to make that non-committal humming noise.

Betsy wasn't deterred. "It's about George."

Wes thought it would be.

"I don't think he understands how much having a baby is going to change our lives," she continued.

Wes considered his response cautiously.

He'd grown up with George and Arthur, who were twin brothers. Arthur was a quality person. He'd stayed in Namur all his life; he and Wes were good friends. In fact, Arthur's dairy farm was right across the street from Wes's cabin. George, on the other hand, had left after graduation and hadn't been back much since. When he did return, he didn't make a good impression. By all appearances, he was still the handsome and reckless cad he'd been in high school.

That wasn't what the mother of his child wanted to hear, though. "Why don't I come around so we can talk more easily," said Wes, trying to buy some time. He hopped out and walked around to the rear of the bus.

Beyond the maple trees, whose buds were swollen near to bursting, the glass doors of the church stood open, letting in the warm afternoon breeze. The lofty building called to him. It would be quiet in there, and Father Tim always had a story to share-nothing personal, just a funny anecdote or joke. How did the priest manage to stay so cheerful? Between him and Ed next door, they'd probably heard more about the trials and tribulations of the people of Namur than Wes ever would. Maybe they could start a support group of sorts: the librarian, the bartender, and the priest.

Ed, a burly biker guy, must have learned to repel confidences with his granite tough exterior. Could Wes develop a similar façade? He narrowed his eyes a bit, in the manner of Ed, and stepped back into the library.

"Did you get a bug in your eye out there?" Betsy asked him, moving to stand. "Here, let me take a look."

Wes abandoned his plan to look less approachable for the time being. He'd have to practice in front of a mirror first. "No need," he said. "I got it." He rubbed his eye and flicked the imaginary bug out the door. "Sneaky little guys. You were saying something about George?"

Betsy nodded. "Ever since I told him I was pregnant, he's been acting really excited about the baby on the rare occasion that I talk to him on the phone, but he hasn't been back since Christmas."

"Is he still in Minneapolis?"

"He is. He says he's working on a big project, developing some kind of shopping center. I don't see why he couldn't stop by on the weekends, though."

Wes didn't know what to say. He wasn't impressed with the guy. "It would mean a lot to you if he was more involved." Wes paraphrased the gist of what she'd said, a technique he'd picked up when he'd done a bit of research on counseling techniques of his own accord. Somehow his library science degree hadn't prepared him for this aspect of the job.

"Yes. See, you get it. I've been lucky; my family has really stepped up. Chloe's helping me prepare the nursery, and my mom went with me for the ultrasound."

"I hear you're having a girl. Congratulations."

Betsy pressed her hands to her stomach and grinned. "Thanks. We're going to be alright, her and me."

"I know you are." Wes meant it too. Betsy had been a bit wild in her younger years, but she always meant well, which Wes had begun to value more highly the older he got.

"Bea's lucky. You're one of the good ones."

"So are you. George is the one missing out."

"Thanks for listening." Betsy's face looked clearer, her shoulders more relaxed. She didn't bother grabbing a book before she left. She'd clearly just been there to talk.

Right as she pulled out of the parking lot, an old blue Civic pulled in with Nick behind the wheel.

"Wes! Guess what?" Nick asked as he jumped into the bookmobile. He didn't wait for Wes to guess. "I got that engineering scholarship, the one I was telling you about last time. They just called to let me know."

"Wow. Congratulations. That was a big one."

"It was. Now I'm sure I'll be able to go. Between that, what my parents and I were able to save, and the help I'll get from my brother, it's all going to work out."

"You'll do great. I can't wait to hear what you think of college life. Let me know when you get your dorm assignment."

"Will do. I'm grabbing some books to read for fun to celebrate. Any recommendations?"

Wes hesitated. Even recommending books felt like giving advice. Books could change lives; as a librarian, he really believed that, and he didn't want to meddle. He liked suggesting books for kids, but adults? He'd prefer if they made their own selections. Fortunately, Nick had moved on and was thumbing through a new fantasy.

"I'll go with this one." Nick handed it over to Wes. "I've got to head to work. The grocery store gets busy in the afternoons, so Mrs. Martel asked me to come in early."

Wes checked out his book, congratulated Nick again on his scholarship win, and bid him farewell. The bookmobile would start to get busy soon too, and that would mean crowds. Crowds meant less privacy, and less privacy meant fewer people able to divulge their deepest secrets without others listening in. Wes sat down on a stool and pulled out a middle grade book he'd been considering as an addition to the library's collection. It would be smooth sailing from here on out.

The peace lasted less than five minutes.

Coming from outside, an angry yell broke Wes's concentration. As he slapped his book shut and set it down on the shelf, ready to tell whoever it was to pipe down, a heavy thud against its side rocked the bookmobile. The yelling got louder. Wes sprang up from his seat, sprinted out of the bus, and gasped. A man sprawled, unconscious, across the hot black asphalt.

Chapter Two

In Which a Handsome Stranger Dines In

"Back already?" Chloe asked from her seat at the table when Betsy walked into the kitchen. Marshmallow, Chloe's massive chocolate lab, groaned from beneath a chair and shifted positions.

Betsy sat down across from her sister and switched on her laptop. There was sure to be a new batch of e-mails waiting to be tackled. "I ran over to the bookmobile for a second."

"Find anything good?"

Betsy shrugged. "Not really."

Chloe probably suspected that Betsy had gone there to talk to Wes. He was becoming famous for his skills at helping people sort out their love lives, and it wasn't exactly a secret that Betsy's could use some sorting. She felt better after talking to him, but she wasn't any closer to knowing what to do about George.

It had seemed so romantic when George came back at Christmas. She'd told him about the baby, and he acted over the moon at the news that he was going to be a father. They'd taken a drive up north to look at cribs and sweet little handmade clothes, but once he'd gone and the thrill of the holidays had passed, she realized that he'd never committed to being around more. They'd never talked about what his role would be in their baby's life-or Betsy's, for that matter.

Betsy didn't know what she wanted his role to be either, so she couldn't exactly come down on him for it, but a little more clarity than none would've been nice.

"Business sure is booming," said Chloe from her side of the table. "I knew spring would be busy, but this is really something."

Betsy scanned her inbox: thirty new e-mails in the hour she was gone. "At this rate you're going to need to hire another employee."

"I don't know about that. I want to keep it in the family."

"Maybe Mom would give up the salon and become your second customer service rep."

"Can you imagine? She'd try to convince our women farmers that ergonomic tools aren't all they're cracked up to be. What they really want is a nice manicure and some highlights. She almost fainted when she ran into me on Main Street yesterday."

Chloe's nails were cracked and dirty, her hair pulled into a messy braid that ran down her back. Wisps of blonde locks stuck out around her face. Between the start of gardening season and her burgeoning business, she clearly hadn't been making personal hygiene a priority. "Hey," she said, looking up from her pile of papers, "why don't we go over to Emma's tonight for dinner? My treat. It'll give me an excuse to clean up a bit."

Betsy would've loved nothing more than to have a seat in one of the plush benches by the window at the end of a long day. She'd order a juicy burger and thick crispy fries, but it would have to remain a fantasy. "I promised Emma I'd work tonight."

"You've been putting in a lot of time there. You know I consider you full-time now. We're doing great. I'm sure I'll be able to give you a raise soon."

"That'll be fantastic. I must admit, I'm getting pretty tired, but I'm trying to build a little nest egg for when the baby comes. Besides, Emma hasn't hired anyone else to take my place. I don't think she wants to admit I'm moving on, and I don't have the heart to press it."

"Let's plan dinner for another time then." Chloe tried to sound upbeat, but there was a note of concern beneath her breezy reply.

Being the subject of her sister's concern wasn't unfamiliar territory for Betsy. Up until her relationship with George, Betsy had been content to sow her wild oats. She had a reputation for being attracted to bad boys, a reputation she'd wholeheartedly earned. If he had a motorcycle, a criminal record, a love of extreme sports, or any combination of those three, a man suddenly became that much more desirable.

Chloe, on the other hand, went for silly shenanigans and practical jokes. Come to think of it, Betsy wasn't entirely certain which one of them had made more trouble over the years, but Betsy's brand of trouble had resulted in more significant consequences.

Those days were all behind her now, and Betsy couldn't say she was sorry to see them go. She'd had her fun, but she was looking forward to settling down and focusing on things that were more meaningful, things that would last. She turned back to her e-mails and burst out laughing.

"Did you get another one from Gadgetgal?" Chloe asked.

"Yes. This is the fifth one I've gotten in five days."

"Ooh, let's see." Chloe scooted around Betsy's chair to read the latest testimonial.

"It's for the pruning shears."

What can I say about these shears that hasn't already been said about sliced bread, modern dentistry, or the smart phone? They changed my life, first for the better, then for the worse, then for the better again. I enjoyed using them so much that I lopped all the limbs off my cherry trees. Considering converting my orchard into a world-class cross country slalom ski course. Thanks so much Bare Roots Tools!

"This is totally your sense of humor," said Betsy, eyeing up Chloe with suspicion.

"I wish I'd have thought of it, but it's not me. I swear."

"Well whoever it is, they've been making my day. They're hilarious."

"Mine too. I hope they keep it up."

"Did you see yesterday's?" Betsy scanned her screen until she found another review from the same sender.

If I could give your shovel a one-thousand-star rating, I would. At first, I only used it for the obvious: digging ditches, planting squash, and beheading sneaky cobras. I soon found, however, that it could also replace my boyfriend, who had the gall to suggest that I was delusional (because of the seeing cobras everywhere thing). A magic marker and a smiley face on the head were all it took for the shovel to become my new mister right. He doesn't smell, he's happy to sleep in the shed, and he never asks to borrow my car. His name's Dirk.

"Dirk the shovel," Chloe mused. "Maybe we've unearthed our new mascot. Unearthed. Get it? Because he's a shovel?"

Betsy didn't justify that with a response. "This really isn't you?" she asked. Chloe had named her truck Old Blue, and she talked to it as if they were best pals.

"It's really not. It's someone channeling my spirit."

"Fair enough, I believe you," Betsy said, but she kept an eye on Chloe for the rest of the day.

They worked until dinner-time. It had become a tradition for them to make dinner together, but Betsy had to run if she wanted to be in time for her shift at the cafe.

"You're leaving without eating?" Chloe looked up from chopping peppers at the counter while Betsy gathered her things and pushed away from the table.

"I have a salad in the fridge at home. I'll grab it on my way. Don't worry. I'm taking good care of myself."

"OK. I don't mean to be bugging you again, but it's part of the older sister job description. You know I'm not one to slack off."

"It doesn't bother me." In fact, Betsy appreciated having someone looking out for her.

"Good. Because I'd do it anyway."

Betsy knew she would. She said goodbye to Chloe and headed down the sidewalk and back to her house, where she wolfed down her hard-boiled egg topped arugula salad. She glanced at the clock. If she hurried, she'd make it just in time for the dinner crowd.

When Betsy got to the cafe it was still relatively quiet.

"Thanks for coming in again," Emma said, catching her breath while she smoothed the black bun perched on top of her head. "Look at you! We're going to have to find a bigger apron for you pretty soon. I can't wait to have a toddler running around here." She ran away with a tray of ice waters balance in her hand as though the rush was already on.

Betsy tied a black and white checkered apron around her waist and tucked a notepad and pencil into the front pocket.

A man in a baseball cap, fitted green t-shirt, and dark jeans sat down in one of the far booths with his back to her. It looked like he'd just arrived. It also appeared, by his confident swagger and the way his t-shirt hugged his arms, that he was exactly the kind of guy who would've appreciated the old Betsy's flirtatious banter. The new Betsy wasn't particularly trying to notice that; it was just particularly noticeable. She would take his order then ask Emma what section of the café she should cover once things got busier.

As Betsy approached his table, the man pulled off his cap and set it next to him on his seat. There was only one person she knew with dark red hair like that. The guy was Karl? How had she not recognized him? This was the first time she'd seen him in a t-shirt since last fall. Betsy felt her face growing hot.

"Oh, hey. I didn't know you'd be waitressing tonight." Karl smiled up at her. He must've come straight from the shop. A smear of grease shone on his prominent freckled cheekbone, just above his beard. Had his eyes always been that deeply aqua?

Betsy cleared her throat. "Yup. I'm still helping out every now and then."

"Well, you're looking great."

"Thanks. So are you. It's always good to see you."

"You too. Pregnancy suits you."

"It's nice of you to say so. It's starting to get a little uncomfortable. And when I said you were looking great, I meant...have you been working out? You're not pregnant, of course." She glanced around the café. Why wasn't anyone coming by to stop her from carrying on with this embarrassing display?

"Nope, not yet, anyway." He patted his stomach

and chuckled to himself. Karl was just like Chloe, always cracking himself up. "I have been working out, though. I'm trying to get your dad to join me, but the boss isn't having it. I don't want to push my luck with him. Thank you for noticing my efforts."

"Oh, I wasn't noticing, like, *noticing.* I just…Are you meeting anyone tonight?"

"Why, do you want to join me?"

"I wish I could, but I was actually wondering if I should take your order now or wait a bit."

"I know; I was kidding. Are you alright? You're looking a little flushed."

"Yeah. This happens all the time." *Whenever I'm near you.* "It's a weird pregnancy thing." *I'm actually pretty sure it's not.*

"And here I was thinking it was just the effect I have on the ladies."

Betsy laughed; it came out as a snort. Why was she being so weird? They were two friends who'd known each other since they were babies, joking around like they always did. In the last year though, Betsy had started picking up on some worrying developments on the Karl front.

Such as: face growing hot whenever she was near him, awkward laughter (from her), a delicious manly smell (from him, obviously), and a growing awareness of how much she'd always preferred men with beards.

Thankfully, Karl had remained oblivious so far.

"I'm going to eat here," he said, "but then I'd like to get something to go for Nick. He had to work at the grocery store tonight, but he got that scholarship he was hoping for. I want to surprise him with dinner."

"Oh wow. That's so exciting. Tell him congratulations for me. Your parents must be so proud." Betsy tapped the pen against her notepad, matching the frantically fluttering pulse racing just beneath her collarbone.

"They really are. I am too. Nick's the brains in the family. He'll be the first one of us to go to college. He wants to be an engineer, like Chloe."

"That's great. Tell him to stop by any time if he wants to check out her business. It's really interesting, even to me. She has a crazy workshop in the garage too. I don't know what half her tools are even for. I'm forbidden from touching them, but she might let Nick try some things out."

"I bet he'd love that."

"You might want to warn him to make sure he plans to make a day of it. Once Chloe gets talking about tool design and materials and stuff, she can't stop."

"That sounds perfect. He'll probably be on her front porch first thing tomorrow morning."

"I'll keep an eye out for him."

Karl ordered his food, and Betsy soon returned with a glass of water. Karl rarely ate in the café, but when he did, he always kept it simple. He was a single guy without any responsibilities except a little house just down the road from Betsy's, but he never did anything extravagant, and that included not ordering anything more than ice water to drink.

"Thanks," he said, taking a big gulp from the tall plastic cup. "It's been crazy at the shop. Must be a full moon this week, because everyone's cars are going haywire."

"Good to hear it's not just mine," Betsy said.

"What do you mean?"

"Oh nothing, it's fine. The brakes are a little squeaky, but it's probably just the humidity." She hadn't meant to say anything about her car's quirks. Her dad would fix it for free if she asked, but Betsy didn't want to ask. She also didn't want to spend the money on fixing it unless she absolutely had to.

"If you think there's something wrong, you should have it looked at. I wouldn't mind checking it out any time. In fact, why don't you give me the keys now? I'll take it for a test drive after I eat."

Betsy would've preferred if no one checked it out. What she didn't know wouldn't hurt her, right? But even as she thought it, she knew she was being irresponsible. If Karl found something, she could decide whether it was important enough to fix. She'd just have to ask him not to say anything to her dad.

"It's probably fine, but if it isn't, I'll make you a deal." Karl lowered his voice and moved over, patting the seat next to him.

Betsy slid in close. Beneath the smell of frying butter and charred burgers came the scent of engine oil, cinnamon, and citrus. Her skin prickled where their arms touched, and Betsy edged away.

As usual, Karl didn't seem to notice. The little bit of luck she had was holding. "If there's something up with your brakes," he said, "-and from the sound of it, your brake pads are probably worn-I can fix it after hours. I don't want to make assumptions, but I'm guessing you don't feel comfortable asking for help from your dad."

Betsy gulped and nodded. "How do you always know?"

"You'd be amazed how much you can learn about people by snooping in their glove boxes."

Betsy laughed for real this time, slapping him playfully on the shoulder. It was firmer than she remembered. "You don't really do that."

He nudged her; that prickly feeling travelled up her arm and along her neck. What was that about? "You're right," he said. "I don't, but I'd be happy to help you."

"I don't want to take advantage."

"You're not. I'm offering."

Ugh. He was so thoughtful, too. "Wouldn't you have to buy the brake pads?"

"Yeah, but that would be the only cost. Like I said, don't worry about it. I'll take a look."

"What are we talking about?" George slid into the booth on the other side of them and pulled off his sunglasses. He gave Betsy his most winning smile then turned his gaze to Karl and dimmed it down just enough to create a look that was more challenging than friendly. Karl smiled back thinly.

Betsy's eyes darted back and forth between the two of them. Tall dark and scowling versus tall red and beardy. She shook her head and snapped out of it. "George? Oh my gosh. What are you doing here? I didn't know you were coming up." She got up and came around to George's side. He put his arm around her, pulling her in close, and kept it there.

"I wanted to surprise you. I hope I wasn't interrupting anything."

"Not at all. I was just about to grab Karl's food. In fact, I think it's ready back there." Betsy hopped up; George followed behind her.

He took a seat at a stool by the counter, where he straightened the collar on his crisp Oxford shirt and smoothed out his navy shorts. He checked his watch like he was already bored. "What are you up to this weekend? I thought we might be able to take a drive up the peninsula tomorrow and check out the cherry blossoms."

"I have a Demeter Society meeting in the morning, and I promised Chloe I'd help her get ready for an agriculture expo in the afternoon. Would Sunday work?"

"Wow. You're working overtime." He sounded more annoyed than impressed, but Betsy chose to take it as a compliment.

"I guess I *am* in pretty high demand. Did you just decide to come up?" A little warning would've been helpful if he really wanted to do something with her.

"Yeah. It was a last-minute thing."

"It's no problem, but would Sunday be alright?" she asked again.

George pulled out his phone, probably checking his calendar. "Sure. Sunday might work, if I don't have to leave early. I just got a new car. If it's warm enough, we could leave the top down."

A bumblebee yellow Porsche convertible sat right outside the café's big bay window. Betsy's eyes widened. Last year, George had been planning to build a shopping center and apartment complex on Main Street. He left Namur instead, claiming he'd decided that it wasn't a good investment. Betsy had suspected he'd run into financial difficulties, but maybe that wasn't the case after all.

"It's a bit flashy," he said, "but it's important for me project an image of success."

Betsy, who had turned her back to him in order to grab Karl's plate, held back the impulse to roll her eyes. George was so intent on being admired or envied or...she didn't know what. What Betsy would admire is him taking an interest in their baby.

"It's a really nice car. I don't know much about them, but I'm sure my dad would be impressed. I'll be right back." She carried Karl's food over and set it down in front of him. "Do you want anything else?"

"No thanks," he said.

Betsy glanced back at George, who was staring down the two of them. The moment he noticed Betsy looking at him, he turned around and put his glasses on with a flourish.

"Sorry about that," Betsy whispered. "I'm not sure how to take him sometimes."

Karl shrugged it off. "Don't worry about it. You're doing great, and this food looks delicious."

"Okay. Well, thanks, and enjoy." Betsy, who

would've preferred to stay with Karl, headed back over to talk to George.

"I've gotta run," George said, patting her on the shoulder. "I'll be in touch about Sunday." He hopped off the stool, strode out the door, letting it slam behind him, and squealed out of the parking lot.

The next hour went by in a blur as diners started to arrive in earnest. Betsy took one half of the café while Emma took the other. Although the work was becoming more exhausting as her belly expanded, it was also pretty fun, especially on nights like tonight when lots of people she knew came in.

Karl left before Betsy had a chance to talk to him about her car. Bussing his table, Betsy found a note beneath his plate.

I didn't want to distract you while you were busy. Please stop by my house after work so I can take a look at your brakes. I'll be up.

He'd added a twenty-dollar tip to his twenty dollar check.

Chapter Three

In Which Karl Receives a Worrying Message

Karl drove home in a barely controlled rage that took him by surprise. He fought the urge to smash down on the accelerator, and instead turned up his radio and ground his teeth. What was wrong with George? He had the most beautiful girl in town, and he hardly ever showed up. Apparently when he did, he expected her to drop everything just because he'd decided to return.

Karl hadn't meant to eavesdrop on their conversation at the café counter, but George's lazy arrogant voice wasn't exactly difficult to miss. Karl hadn't been sure if the supposed real estate mogul and Betsy were together, but based on the possessive way George had acted when he walked into the diner, it appeared that they were.

Karl shouldn't care about what Betsy was up to, and he knew it. He'd been worrying about her for years, and it never seemed to have any effect beyond making him miserable. Besides, he had other things to think about. Not his own love life in particular-his last relationship had fizzled out ages ago-but surely there were other things that were worthy of his attention. It was even possible that if he stopped comparing everyone else to Betsy, he might be able to eke out a relationship that lasted longer than a couple of months.

Karl pulled into his driveway and cut the engine. He snatched the Styrofoam container of food off the passenger seat and stomped into the house. Flopping down onto the couch, he waited for his brother to come through the front door. Nick would cheer him up. He was an eternal optimist, even after everything they'd been through.

As if on cue, Nick strolled through the door and stepped into the living room, whistling a jaunty tune. "Whoa. Am I interrupting something?"

"No. What do you mean?"

"You're lying on the couch listening to angsty music alone on a Friday night. You never do that."

"What? Lie on the couch or listen to angsty music?"

"Both."

"I was tired, and this song just happened to come on." The anguished strains of an 80s ballad flowed from Karl's speakers. It was actually pretty depressing and happened to fit his mood perfectly.

"If you say so."

"I do. Hey, wait here a minute." Karl rolled off the couch onto the floor, jumped up, switched off the music, and ran into the kitchen. Moments later, he came back out with a plate full of reheated café food.

"No way. Just when I thought this day couldn't get any better. Are those Emma's fries?" Nick crossed the room in two steps and took the plate out of Karl's hand.

"Come on, let's go into the kitchen."

They sat down at the table, and Karl watched with satisfaction as Nick wolfed down his BLT. He couldn't believe that kid's appetite. Nick was already taller than Karl, and he didn't seem to have any plans of slowing down.

"How'd it go at the grocery store tonight?" Karl asked.

"Oh, you know how it is," said Nick through a bite of his sandwich, "lots of intrigue, conspiracies, titillating rumors."

"What is it about that place?"

"I don't know. It's probably something about the combined smell of donuts and bleach that captivates people. Did you hear George is back? He stopped in tonight."

"Yeah. I saw him at the cafe."

"Wait a minute," said Nick, jabbing a fry at his brother. "I think I'm putting something together: café food, George, existential angst...was Betsy working tonight?"

Karl slapped the table with a comically dramatic thud. "Hey, way to go on that scholarship."

They both laughed. "Okay. Fine, I won't ask, but if it makes you feel better, George came into the grocery store and asked Mrs. Martel if all of our cheeses were 'hand selected'. What does that even mean? What other options are there? Selecting them by foot? Closing your eyes and picking whatever one you end up pointing at? It's one of those things people say to sound fancy that doesn't really mean anything."

"What did Mrs. Martel say?"

"She said yes, of course. She's probably having a sign made up as we speak. She's always talking about catering to her 'up-market customers'."

"Thanks. That does make me feel better." There was a knock at the front door. "That's probably Betsy. I said I'd take a look at her car."

"I bet you did."

"What's that supposed to mean?" Karl laughed.

"It isn't supposed to mean anything. It *does* mean that you two are obsessed with each other. Why don't you just get together already?"

"I think she's with George."

"Mister 'hand selected'? You think? Why don't you know?"

"They broke up a while ago, but he didn't look very happy to see me talking to her tonight. They have plans tomorrow, too."

"So, ask her if they're back together."

"We don't talk about that stuff. We never have."

"Why not?"

"I'm answering the door now. That's going to need to stop."

"Fine, I'm willing to keep quiet."

"Gee, thanks."

"But only because you brought me my favorite meal."

Shaking his head, Karl opened the door to Betsy, who was shivering on his front porch. "Come on in. You look freezing." He led her into the kitchen.

"It got really chilly tonight." She rubbed her arms. She spotted Nick at the table and congratulated him on his scholarship.

"News got around fast," he said.

"Everyone's thrilled for you."

"Thanks. That means a lot." Nick stood up from the table. "I've gotta run. It'll be another early day tomorrow, but it was good seeing you, Betsy." Nick gave his brother an eyebrow wiggle, which was met with a warning glare. He headed to his car, leaving Karl and Betsy alone in the kitchen.

Betsy twisted the tarnished silver ring on her middle finger and bit her lower lip. It seemed like there was something going on with her. She was usually so outgoing and gregarious, but tonight she seemed almost shy. He'd noticed it at the diner too. Was she really that worried about some squeaky brakes, or was there more to it than that? Good thing the subject of her car had come up so Karl could help her out.

"Do you want to take a drive with me?" he asked. "Otherwise, you can stay here and warm up if you want to. I'll just be going around the block."

Betsy brightened up. "I'll come with you. We can cruise around the neighborhood. It'll be like old times." She handed him her keys.

"Just a second. Let me grab you one of my sweatshirts." Karl ran into his bedroom and pulled the softest one he could find off his floor. He gave it a quick sniff and, deeming it acceptable, carried it back out to Betsy.

She slipped it on over her dress and followed him out the door.

Inside the car, Karl backed onto the road. He hit the brakes. *Squeak*. That sound was much more definitive than he'd been expecting. "How long have they been doing this?"

"A while," Betsy said, glancing away with a grimace.

"Yeah. You need new brake pads right away. You shouldn't have let them go this long."

Betsy groaned, leaning back against the head-rest.

"It's a quick fix," Karl assured her. "Bring it around to the shop Monday night after your dad closes up. I'll be waiting for you. It'll take no time, and they'll be good as new. You'll also be guaranteed to be able to stop when you want to. I know that might not seem like that big of a deal to a layperson, but as a mechanic, I can tell you it's one of the more important things to be able to do with a car."

"Ha ha." Betsy smiled at him and gave him an-other whack of the shoulder. Had she just squeezed it a little? "You think you're so clever."

"Please, I know I am." He turned serious. Seeing Betsy snuggled into his sweatshirt wasn't dimming his protective instincts in the least. "Just come over on Monday and have your car fixed, alright?"

"I will. I promise. You won't get into trouble, will you? What if my dad finds out?"

"He won't, but if he did, I'm sure he wouldn't

mind me helping you."

"I really don't want him to know. I keep messing up, and I don't want him to think I'm struggling. I've given him enough to worry about over the past few years."

"No one will know. I promise."

Arriving back home, Karl got out of the car and left it running. Betsy ran around from the other side and wrapped him in a hug, kissing him on the cheek. Now that was more like the Betsy he knew. Her car troubles must've been weighing on her that much.

"Monday around six?" she asked.

"Make it 6:30. It'll be quieter on Main Street then."

"Ooh. It's like we're planning a secret rendezvous."

"We are."

"I love it. Thanks again. Good night."

"See you," he said, waving as she drove away. She'd forgotten to give him back his sweatshirt. Oh well, they'd see each other again soon.

Back in the house, Karl picked up his phone. He had a text from Betsy's dad. That had almost never happened, unless there was something wrong. He wasn't a chatty guy, in person or on the phone.

Come in early Monday. Need to talk.

Well, that was ominous. Dare he respond and ask what they needed to discuss? Karl thought back through the past couple of weeks. Nothing stood out as a problem, but he couldn't be sure.

True, Karl had a little trouble keeping it together when that woman had come in with her Prius, but he didn't think she'd picked up on his amusement amidst her blustering indignation.

She'd brought the car in last week, complaining that it wasn't running well. Karl took it for a drive and had to agree. The car was only two years old, and it rattled down the road like the engine was almost shot. She'd put a lot of miles on it, but not that many. He asked her when she'd last had her oil changed.

"It's a Prius." She enunciated both syllables with forced exaggeration.

That was true. It was a Prius. He waited for what was sure to be an interesting explanation.

"It doesn't need oil changes," she said.

He furrowed his brow in confusion. The woman sighed like he was just too much to take.

"It does need oil changes," he said, "just like any other car."

The woman scoffed. "It doesn't have an engine."

"It doesn't have a..."

"An engine. It doesn't have an engine. What would the oil be for?"

"It does have an engine."

"It's an *electric* car. I heard this was an honest establishment. Are you new here? I want to talk to the owner."

"It's a hybrid, and it's a very nice car, but it does have an engine."

She pursed her lips and tapped her foot as she

waited for him to locate a competent mechanic: one who knew a thing or two about which cars had engines and which ones did not.

"I'll be right back," he'd said, valiantly maintaining a professional exterior. He held up alright until he reached the front office and started explaining to Frank that he needed to convince a customer that her car had an engine.

"Yup," said Frank, sauntering out of the office without even cracking a smile.

That night after work, Karl stopped at his parents' house to ask Nick if it was just him who thought it was funny. Nick could hardly keep it together enough to respond.

"Nope, there's no excuse. That's hilarious. You were so nice about it, too. You're way too nice, you know."

"So I've been told, but what was I supposed to do?"

"Was her car okay?"

"Yeah. It'll be fine. She wouldn't believe Frank either, but then he showed her the engine, and that kind of ended the argument. I could tell she still thought we were up to something, though."

"You are up to something. Telling people their cars have engines..." Nick shook his head in disgust.

"She'll have to warn people about us. I doubt we'll ever see her again. That has to sink in as being embarrassing eventually."

"I don't know, sometimes people don't see things, even when the evidence is right in front of them."

Back at home, Karl drafted a message to Frank then erased it. Frank had fired a string of mechanics before Karl because they'd been too chatty or made too much of an effort to befriend him. Frank would never admit that was the reason he'd let them go, but everyone in the village knew it was true. Karl had almost made the mistake of inviting Frank to deer camp last fall, until Chloe warned him about the pitfalls of making such an overture.

If Karl responded, Frank might feel pressure to write back. He wouldn't like that. Karl should say something though, if only to let him know he'd gotten the message and would be there.

See you then.

That was simple enough. Yes. Simple and to the point. Now Karl had the whole weekend to worry about that text. Frank almost never asked him to come in early, and the one time he did, they got right to work; they certainly didn't talk.

Oh no.

Could Frank be getting ready to fire him, too?

Karl paced the floor. He needed this job. Aside from the obvious reasons like buying food and paying his mortgage, Nick was counting on him. It would've been a stretch for Nick to go to college without his brother's help. Karl was more than happy to do it, but it left him with a new sense of responsibility that he hadn't had when he was just looking out for himself. Something was going on, and whatever it was, Karl was already sure he wasn't going to like it.

He grabbed his car keys and headed for the door. Sitting around here wondering what was going to happen in three days wasn't doing him any favors. He'd go over to Ed's Tavern and see if any of the guys were out tonight. He played darts with a bunch of them on Wednesdays, mostly because it was the quietest night of the week at the bar, but it could be fun to be there when there was more of a crowd. If it wasn't fun, it would at the very least be distracting.

Monday would come soon enough.

Chapter Four

In Which a Friendly Game of Pool Turns Ugly

Wes waded through the fog of cigarette smoke in front of Ed's Tavern, holding his breath until he was inside. Once the door closed behind him, he exhaled and scanned the room. Just as he'd suspected, there was no sign of Arthur or his brother George anywhere. He hadn't seen Arthur's truck in the lot, and he couldn't remember what George drove. Nothing suitably impractical had stood out amongst the modest Fords and Chevys parked outside.

The bar was busy tonight. A group of guys played pool in the corner, and a crowd sat and stood around the bar. The smell in here was a bit better than it had been outside, but only marginally so. It smelled the way it always did: flat beer, sweaty bodies, and something sickly sweet, the source of which Wes preferred not to think about.

Wes found an open stool at one end of the bar and took a seat. How had he ended up getting roped into coming here? He could be back at home right now, lying in bed with a book or sitting around a roaring bonfire with Bea. He could be drinking good beer instead of the cup of corn colored liquid that had just been plopped in front of him. It was rumored that Ed watered down his already homely brews, but Wes had never met anyone brave enough to call him out on it.

If he got a chance tonight, Wes was going to ask the gruff bartender how he handled the responsibility of knowing everyone's stories. Wes considered him, standing behind the bar, wiping out a glass with a dirty rag that he'd just used to wipe the counter.

Ed wore a bandana all the time. Wes had never seen him without one. Tonight it was black and orange. His gray beard hung down to his chest, a long and scraggly mop. Tattoos covered both his forearms and the backs of his hands. He had a look on his face that was so unapproachable it was a marvel to Wes. Wes would have to work long and hard to achieve that level of surliness.

No one would make the mistake of thinking *Ed* had a bug in his eye.

"Hey Ed," Wes called over to him.

Ed didn't appear to have heard him at first, but then he turned slowly and trained his piercing gray eyes on Wes. Wes imagined what Ed must think of him. Wes was tall but rather slight and was working on a goatee. He'd worn his glasses tonight, the ones that had looked so stylish in Madison but somehow made him feel like a bit of a nerd amongst the other locals.

"You need something?" Ed asked blandly.

"I have a question for you."

Ed shook his head and went back to wiping out the pint glass. It looked from here like all he was accomplishing was making it dirtier, but who was Wes to say? He wasn't the bartender. Just when Wes was certain he was going to carry on ignoring him, Ed asked, "Is it about the beer?"

"No," Wes said. "It's about..." People stopped talking and glared at the guy at the end of the bar who had dared to disturb the barkeep. Wes got up and came around so he was close enough that he wouldn't have to shout. "It's about something else."

"I don't discuss anything else."

"See? That's perfect!"

"What is?"

"That's exactly what I wanted to ask you about: not discussing anything."

"You've lost me."

"I've been driving the bookmobile for a while. People like to come in and talk to me about their issues and get my advice. Does that happen to you, too?"

"Sometimes."

"So, what do you do about it?"

"What do I do about what?"

"What do you do about people coming to you with their problems? It's overwhelming, and they tell me things I'd rather not know. Do you try to help them? And then if you do, what if your advice isn't any good? Before I moved here, I worked in a law library at a university; I've never run into this sort of thing."

Ed snorted. "I'll tell you what. If you're still here at closing time, I'll tell you exactly what I do about it. If you're not, let's not mention this again. Understood?"

Those were odd stipulations; Wes hadn't planned on staying that long. "When's closing time?"

"It's when I tell everyone to get the hell out."

Wes had to respect Ed's attitude. He was going to stay as long as it took. "Deal. I'll be here."

"I'm only doing this because you helped me out with those guys this afternoon. Sorry about that, by the way. Is your bus alright?"

"It's fine," said Wes. Incredibly, a flying body hadn't dented it. "They don't make mobile libraries like they used to."

"I thought those knuckleheads would stop fighting once they'd gotten some fresh air and cooled down. They didn't." Ed shrugged and went back to his cleaning.

Someone sat down next to Wes. It was Arthur. George wasn't with him.

"My brother's on the phone with some model he met in Minneapolis," Arthur explained. "Or, he says she's some kind of model. I'm really not sure. He said he'd be right behind me."

Someone next to them cleared his throat. It was Karl.

"Hey, you didn't beg Karl to come out tonight too, did you?" Wes asked Arthur.

"No," said Karl. "I just happened to stop in. Why? What's special about tonight? I never see either of you guys in here."

"George insisted that we come," said Arthur. "I

didn't want to, so I asked Wes to meet us. Sometimes George is a lot for me to handle on my own. Last time we were here together he ended up tangoing with Chloe."

"Whoa. Making the moves on your girl." Karl gave Arthur a nudge with his elbow.

"I wasn't worried," Arthur assured him. He took a drink of his beer and made a sour face. Wes assumed he was reacting to the beer, which was particularly typical tonight, and not the thought of twin dancing with his girlfriend.

"You guys want to play pool?" Karl asked. The group that had been playing when Wes walked in was heading out.

"Let's do it." For as little time as Wes spent here, he did love to play. Besides, he needed to stay busy if he was going to stay awake until closing time to talk with Ed.

Just as they were grabbing their cues, George walked through the door with his sunglasses on. He kept them on as he came over to greet his brother and Wes. He gave a brief nod in Karl's direction, and Wes sensed a chill between the two men. It didn't take being the village bookmobile driver to guess what direction that icy breeze was coming from.

"Do you want to play with us?" Wes asked. "We're just starting."

"I'd love to," said George. "But I have to warn you, I'm pretty good."

"Of course you are," Karl said under his breath.

Wes coughed loudly and chalked the end of his

cue. "Why don't Karl and I play first, and then you two can go next."

"Perfect," said Arthur, who, unless he hadn't been paying attention at all, had very likely picked up on the tension between George and Karl as well.

"I say we toss a coin to see who plays first. I wouldn't want to deprive anyone of getting the chance to face off against me." George pulled a quarter out of his pocket and pointed at Karl. "Call it."

"Fine. Heads."

George flipped the coin in the air and slapped it into his palm. "Heads it is. Looks like Karl's playing me."

Wes didn't mind sitting out the first game, but he feared this may not turn out to be the friendliest of matches.

George and Karl stood on opposite sides of the table. George went first. "Funny running into you twice in one day. You go to Emma's often?" George leaned over the table and whacked the cue ball.

"Not really." Karl stared him down with his arms crossed.

"I thought maybe you were a regular."

"Why would you think that?"

"You and Betsy were sitting pretty close in that booth. I'm not worried about it. Don't start flattering yourself with the idea that I see you as competition in any way. I was just curious what was going on between you two." George shot again.

Wow. George wasn't wasting any time in making the night awkward. Wes and Arthur tensed and darted glances between each other and the two rivals. Wes racked his brain for something to say, but he couldn't think of anything that might diffuse the tension. He couldn't look away, either.

"Nothing's 'going on'," said Karl. "We're friends. I look out for her."

"You don't have to sound so defensive. Like I said, I couldn't care less."

"Well, maybe you should care more." Karl hadn't hesitated in his cool response.

George looked up from lining up his shot. "What's that supposed to mean?"

"Do I really need to spell it out for you?"

They'd stopped playing. Both men gripped their cues as if they'd like nothing more than to start fencing with them or, even better, just whack each other over the head and get it over with.

"Funny thing you guys," said Wes. "Whenever I play pool I enforce a pretty strict no talking rule." He widened his eyes at Arthur and nodded, imploring him to step in with some backup.

"Yup," Arthur chimed in. "It's distracting to the other player if you talk during the game. It's part of the official bar rules."

"I like that rule." George glared at Karl.

"So do I." Karl glared back.

Thus followed the most aggressively restrained game of pool that Wes had ever witnessed. The silence was maintained, but it was a silence that was punctuated with the sharp clank of colliding balls. Karl won when George accidentally sunk the eight ball. A vein on George's temple throbbed, but he puffed out his chest and walked around the table to shake Karl's hand.

"I guess the better man doesn't always win," George muttered as he strode over to the bar and grabbed another drink.

Karl couldn't have missed the jab, but he didn't react. Instead, he handed the cue to Wes saying, "You're up," and stood back to watch the second game.

The second game was considerably more sedate. George had found a group of women at the bar to regale with stories of his adventures, so he was occupied while Arthur and Wes faced off and Karl looked on.

The air of tension that had been hovering around them slowly dissipated, and they were able to enjoy the entire game without anyone nearly coming to blows. They also dropped the no talking rule, as George wasn't paying them any attention. George wandered back over as they were packing up. He was chuckling to himself, presumably recalling his own cleverly worded anecdotes.

"I'm going to head out," he said.

"Already?" Arthur didn't sound sorry in the least.

"You guys can stay, but I've got a lot to do this weekend. I'm working remotely tomorrow, and Betsy and I are heading out on Sunday to admire the cherry blossoms. She's really looking forward to it." He grinned, radiating smug satisfaction.

"I think I'll head out too." Arthur grabbed his hat off a chair in the corner.

"You don't have to follow me out," said George. "You should enjoy your night. You hardly ever do this."

"Farmers are funny like that." Arthur was already heading for the door. "It's the early mornings. See you guys. Let's not do this again any time soon," Arthur whispered to Wes as he passed by.

"Done." Wes agreed wholeheartedly.

Wes glanced at the bar. One of the women from the group that George had been talking to, a tall brunette in a tight white tank top and equally tight jeans, watched George with an eagle eye. When he walked out the door, she waved goodbye to her friends and followed close behind.

Karl didn't appear to have noticed the likely reason for George's abrupt departure. Wes, who was still determined to stay until closing time, joined him at the bar.

He had never spent much time with Karl, but it turned out that he was exactly the kind of person that Wes could easily consider a friend. He shared Wes's quirky sense of humor and his taste in books. They talked for another hour or so, until Karl pushed away from the table saying he was going to head out as well.

"Planning on closing this place down tonight?" he asked Wes.

"It looks like it," Wes said. Karl left Wes sitting at the bar with a few remaining holdouts. It couldn't be much longer until Ed would start shunting people out of there.

It wasn't.

Moments after Karl left, Ed unplugged the grimy Coors Beer waterfall sign that hung behind the bar. Everyone but Wes shuffled out of their seats and ambled out the door.

What had just happened?

Did Ed have a secret sign to let everyone know when to leave without saying a word? Wes shook his head in admiration. This guy was in a league of his own. He'd attained a level of commanding authority that Wes could only dream of as he cowered in his bookmobile and silently begged people to leave.

"Huh. You're still here," Ed observed.

"Yep." Wes propped his elbows on the bar and settled his chin in his hands. He couldn't remember the last time he'd stayed up this late.

Ed sighed, deeply. Apparently he hadn't counted on Wes's unique brand of dogged determination. "I guess you really want to know how I...what was it you said?"

Wes straightened up. This was really happening. He was going to get the inside scoop from a true master. "How do you deal with hearing everyone's problems? They keep coming to me and asking for my advice."

Ed cocked his head. "Like you're doing now?"

"Well yes, I suppose so, but it's become almost everyone in the village at this point. It's like there's this huge weight hanging over my head. I'm carrying it around, and it's threatening to crush me. I don't know how to get out from under it."

"That's a pretty colorful image."

Wes nodded and waited for the bartender to say more. Ed reached for the dirty rag he'd been using earlier instead. It had been balled up in the corner, soaked with beer and a splotch of something purple and chunky. He used it to wipe up a spot on the bar.

Finally, he asked, "Aren't you the guy who had all those imaginary friends when you were growing up here?"

Wes wasn't expecting the conversation to head in this direction. "That's me."

"Had 'em through high school, didn't you?"

Wes slid his elbows off the bar to avoid the sticky rag. "I did."

"They still hanging around?"

"No. They've moved on."

"Huh. Well, real people aren't like your imaginary friends. You don't have that much power over them. People are going to do whatever they're going to do. It really doesn't matter what you tell 'em. Usually, when they start talking about their problems, they're just working them out in front of you. Heck, more than half the time I'm not even listening, and they don't notice a thing."

"So, I should just tune them out and let them figure it out for themselves?"

"Maybe. Or maybe tell them some generic good advice stuff. 'Don't be an idiot' usually works, but don't be too hard on yourself if they end up doing something stupid anyway. That's on them. Trust me,

I've seen some people keep going down a road they knew was bad for them, and there was nothing I was going to be able to do or say to change their course. On the other hand, I've also seen quite a few turn things around, but it wasn't because I passed along some brilliant nugget of wisdom. You just don't have that much power."

"But what about the fact that they're coming to me at all? I don't really want to know some of this stuff."

Ed reached into his back pocket and pulled out a battered wallet. "Have you seen old pictures of me? You're too young to remember this, but I used to be what some might call 'approachable'."

He handed Wes a snapshot of a good looking, clean shaven, smiling man in stonewashed jeans and a colorful striped sweater. "That was me then. This is me now." Ed tugged on his patch covered leather vest. "You might want to start working on your image."

Wes considered his own reflection in the mirror behind the bar. If he dressed up like Ed, all he'd do is bolster his reputation as an odd bookworm doing a biker imitation. He might get some laughs, but it wouldn't intimidate anyone. He'd need to find his own angle to discourage personal confidences.

"Thanks. You've given me a lot to..." The door behind the bar that led to Ed's living room clicked shut behind him. Apparently their interview was at an end.

Wes pushed away from the bar and walked towards the exit. In the quiet of the empty room his shoes made sucking sounds as he lifted and lowered them on the tacky linoleum floor.

Once outside, Wes climbed behind the wheel of his car and flicked on his headlights. The glowing eyes of a startled raccoon stared back at him before disappearing into the shrubs on the side of the church.

The lamps on Main Street were still aglow, illuminating the shuttered shops, but once Wes turned onto the county highway that led to his cabin in the woods, the road became so dark that he could only see the road and the edges of the fields that caught the beam of his lights. A blanket of clouds obscured the nearly full moon. A lonesome feeling washed over him. He wished he could stop by and see Bea, but she would've gone to sleep hours ago. Like Arthur, she needed to be up early for the morning milking.

Bea's farm, Cedar Hollow, was just a little farther down the road. Wes passed his narrow dirt driveway and headed over there anyway. There wasn't a chance that she'd be up, but he'd be able to see the barn and her house, snug and quiet in the wakeful gusty night.

He passed the field between their houses followed by her tall red barn. It appeared black and gray in the darkness. The goats were inside, asleep in the straw warmth of their enclosure. Wes pulled into the driveway next to the farmhouse to turn around. There was a bright light on in the kitchen. Bea's bedroom lamp shone from an upstairs window.

Wes brought the car to a screeching stop and leaped out. The lights shouldn't be on at this time of night. Bea was never up this early, and neither were her elderly parents. Something must be wrong.

Chapter Five

In Which a Mysterious Neighbor Creates a Stir

On Saturday morning, Betsy got up early to go to the farmer's market on Main Street. The chill of the early morning caressed her bare skin as she walked down the sidewalk. She breathed in the scent of mud and green things sprouting from the newly warm earth. After a long and sometimes trying winter, Betsy couldn't help but relish the mellow richness of early summer.

The market, which was held in the church parking lot, was bustling with locals and tourists alike. The growing season had just begun; the produce pickings were slim, but Betsy filled her bag with neon red rhubarb and a thick clump of asparagus that was so tender she snacked on the skinny stalks raw as she perused the farm stands.

Bea sat behind a table topped with goat milk lotion, soap, and cheeses. She beamed when she saw Betsy picking her way through the crowd and called a good morning to her.

"What are you doing out here at this hour?" Bea asked.

"I know, right?" said Betsy. "I'm turning over a new leaf." She admired Bea's selection of lotions.

"Do you want a sample? I just added a citrus one."

Betsy squirted a dollop of the creamy white lotion into her hand. It smelled just like Karl had in the cafe. Was he using Bea's lotion? It took her back to last night, the two of them whispering in the cozy booth and wedged into her squeaky car, the feel of his broad shoulders as she hugged him goodnight.

"What do you think?" Bea asked.

"It's lovely. You've been busy."

Bea smiled, but her eyes looked droopy and sad.

"Are you okay?" Betsy asked.

"Sort of." Bea stacked a tower of lavender soap and sighed. "Not really. My mom woke up in the middle of the night again. I found her in the kitchen. She was dressed and ready to walk out the door, convinced she was late for a doctor's appointment."

"Oh no. I'm so sorry."

"Thanks. Wes happened to be coming home from Ed's and came inside to help me settle her down. He was a huge help. It took us a while, but she eventually went back to sleep. I'm not sure what happened. Dad and I have been trying to help her have a consistent routine at night, but I guess it doesn't always make a difference."

"You've got a lot on your plate."

"I sure do. There's no sleeping in on a dairy farm, so it's tough to have interrupted nights of sleep, but my mom has always been there for me. It's not what any of us would've wanted, but I'm going to be here for her too." She set her lips in a hard line. Bea never backed down from a challenge, but she looked worn and tired.

Betsy came around the table and hugged her. She could feel the ridges of Bea's spine beneath her blouse. She had been looking a bit thin, and her hair lacked its usual luster.

Out of the corner of her eye, Betsy spied George in a tent across from them. He was buying a jar of apricot jam. It must've been for his mom. Apricot was Sarah's favorite.

Betsy caught his eye, and George joined her and Bea beneath the Cedar Hollow Farm tent. He whipped off his glasses and gazed at Betsy as if he'd missed her since he'd seen her last night. He hadn't looked at her like that since they were dating. What had changed since yesterday?

"Funny meeting you here." George lifted Betsy's hand to his mouth and kissed it. He licked his lips. "Lemon?"

"It's Bea's lotion," Betsy said. "She's expanded into lotions and soaps."

George nodded his approval. "Diversifying. Very smart."

"Thanks," said Bea. "It's been an adventure."

"Isn't it always? That's business for you. Speaking of which," he turned back to Betsy, "I'm not going to be able to go on our outing tomorrow after all. Something's come up, and I have to run back to the city this afternoon."

"Oh." Betsy's heart sank. As frustrated as she was with George, she would've liked to have spent more time with him. It could've been their chance to discuss the future and get to know each other better. They were having a baby together, after all, but they'd only been together for a couple of months when she got pregnant. She hadn't known him well before that. He was closer to her sister Chloe's age than her own. He and Chloe had been in the same class growing up. Until last year, he'd never given Betsy the time of day.

What could she do about tomorrow though? It was possible that George was scrambling just as hard as she was to have everything in order when the baby arrived. Maybe he would be more involved after she was born.

"I get it," she said. "Business calls."

"We'll make plans next time I'm up."

"Sounds great. Let me know when that is, okay?" Betsy tried to sound carefree, but she wasn't certain she was pulling it off.

"Yeah, of course." George's phone dinged in his pocket. "Another fire to put out. You'd think I'd be able to leave for a couple of days, but some of these guys don't want to make a single decision on their own. I have to run." He kissed Betsy's hand once again, giving her his most seductive look. What was he up to? "I really am sorry tomorrow didn't work out."

She probably shouldn't, they were just words after all, but Betsy felt better at hearing them. "No worries," she said. "I'm happy your business is going so well."

"I knew you'd understand. You're the best." He

walked away. Betsy watched his retreating back until he was out of sight. She felt Bea watching her in turn.

"Are you coming to the meeting this morning?" Bea asked.

"I wouldn't miss it for the world. Grace and I have been planning the decorations. You guys are going to love our ideas. Well, they're mostly hers, but I helped a little too."

"Can't wait. I might be a little late, depending on how things are going around here."

"I'll let you get back to selling your amazing wares."

"Hey, do you want to take a bottle of lotion? I still need testers."

"Like guinea pigs?"

"Yeah. I think it might be turning people's skin blue, but they're too polite to tell me."

"In that case, I'll take five."

Bea glanced around. "I probably shouldn't joke while I'm trying to sell them. But really, I've been giving out bottles around town. I'm hoping I can get everyone hooked so they'll come back for more."

"Oh. Did you give one to Karl?" Betsy asked nonchalantly, picking up a bar of watermelon soap and giving it a sniff.

"I did. How did you know?"

"Just a lucky guess. I'd love one."

"Did you like the citrus?"

"I loved the citrus." Bea handed her a stout glass bottle of lotion. Betsy pulled off the cap and smelled it again. It smelled like sitting next to a sweet guy in a warm booth at Emma's on a Friday night. "You know what? I'll be back for more anyway. I'll buy this one from you." She handed Bea the twenty-dollar bill Karl had left her.

"You don't have to do that."

"I know, but I want to. I can't imagine all the work that goes into making this." A soft green tag, which hung from the bottle by a piece of twine, said *Made with Love at Cedar Hollow Farm*.

"Well thanks," said Bea as Betsy slid the bottle of lotion into her bag with the rest of her finds.

With a bag full of goodies, Betsy headed home.

****

Two hours later, all the members of the Demeter Society gathered in Lindsay's barn at Cherry Bounce Inn. Betsy and Grace had already started to decorate it for the fundraising fair, and it was looking pretty fabulous already, if Betsy did say so herself.

Overhead, rainbow colored paper lanterns dangled from a lofty ceiling and strings of lights wound around rustic beams. All that was missing were the sheets of colorful fabric that would drape from the wagon wheel chandelier to the far walls on all sides, creating the effect of a giant circus tent.

The six members of the society: Sarah, Bea, Lindsay, Grace, Betsy, and Chloe clustered around one of the round tables.

"The dunk tank is almost finished being built," said Chloe. "But I haven't had much luck finding volunteers."

"Can you blame people?" Bea shivered. "The thought of perching above a tank of cold water, waiting for someone to knock you in..."

"I'm just going to have to do it if no one else wants to." Chloe would probably enjoy that. Betsy could just picture her daring people to knock her in.

"You shouldn't have to, though." Bea objected. "You had to make it."

"I'm sure it won't be that bad. Maybe Arthur will be willing to take turns with me if I start to get too cold."

"I know he will, dear. I was just about to make that suggestion," said Sarah, the oldest member of the society who also happened to be George and Arthur's mom.

It was true. Arthur would do anything for Chloe. He wore his heart on his sleeve and made no secret of how crazy he was about her. Why did Betsy have to pick the flaky twin? Because George was aloof and unattainable, that's why.

"What about the bachelor auction?" Betsy asked. Going on a date with one of the lovely ladies of Door County had to be an easier sell than being plunged into icy water.

"That's gone better than I expected." Chloe rubbed her hands together with a sneaky gleam in her eye.

"Who did you get?"

"Lindsay's neighbor Jack."

Everyone nodded in approval. A date with Jack

would be a coveted prize. He lived on the farm next to Lindsay's, was down-to-earth, and loved his animals. He wasn't hard on the eyes, either. He'd been reported, at Martel's Grocery no less, to be newly single. The rumors must've been true.

"I can't believe he agreed," said Lindsay. "When I talked to him about it a couple of weeks ago, he insisted that no one would be interested in him."

"I may have bribed him with some free tools," Chloe admitted. "But he's wrong about the interest level around here. I let the names of two of our three contestants slip at the café, and I'm pretty sure we're guaranteed a crowd."

"Contestants, you say? Who else did you get?" Grace asked.

"Lucas."

Huh. Interesting choice. Betsy didn't know much about him; he'd moved here only last month following a divorce with the intention of restoring an old Belgian farmhouse that had fallen into disrepair. Like Jack, Lucas was strikingly handsome. Unlike Jack, he was also new to town, which would give him that extra mystery factor.

"No way," said Grace. "How did you manage that?"

"He didn't need any convincing. I told him about our plan to use most of the funds to hire a veteran to work with our businesses, and he said he'd be happy to do it."

"Wow. Two newly single eligible bachelors." Grace looked impressed. "I'd call that a success. You said there were three guys, though."

"Did I?" Chloe grinned.

"You know you did," said Grace.

"I might have said that."

"So, who's the third?" Betsy asked.

"It's a surprise."

Her sister could be so exasperating. "You can't do that."

"Oh, but I am."

"Come on, Chloe."

"It'll be more fun this way."

"Fun for you, maybe."

"Fun for you, too. I'm not telling anyone. The intrigue will draw more of a crowd. Trust me."

"I've heard that before."

"And I always come through." Betsy couldn't argue with that.

"Are we allowed to make a bid?" Sarah asked jokingly. She and Roy had been married for decades, with five children and a posse of grandchildren to show for it.

"Go for it," Chloe said. "I'm advertising all over the county though, so you're going to have some stiff competition."

"This is be so much fun." Betsy didn't have money to spend on buying a date or the slightest interest in going on one, but it would be a blast to watch.

"What else do we have going on?" Lindsay asked. "Jack'll bring his horse over and give wagon rides. We've got ring toss, a rubber duck kiddie pool with prizes, the DJ is booked, and I've got the menu all figured out."

"Will you have any guests here that weekend?" Sarah asked.

Lindsay nodded. "Three women will be up for a bachelorette weekend. One of them has stayed here before. She's going to have her wedding in the barn in August."

"Do you think she'll want a circus theme?" Grace asked. "If she does, we'll be all set." Grace, Lindsay's sister, had been decorating for all of their events. Her touch for creating the perfect mood was becoming the talk of the village. Some outside venues were hiring her out to decorate their event halls as well.

"I kind of doubt it, but you never know," said Lindsay. "Remember those people who wanted a bacon themed wedding?"

"Umm...yes. I still have the bacon tablecloths in case it comes up again. Maybe you and Harvey will settle on a breakfast foods theme for your wedding too."

Lindsay shuddered. "Not in a million years. Moving on, does anyone else have anything they want to add?"

No one did.

They stayed for another hour just to chat, until Betsy and Chloe had to leave so Chloe could get ready for her conference.

On the ride home, Betsy admired the fields full of cherry trees that lined the county highway. They were all in bloom, their white petals coating the ground like a late dusting of snow.

Too bad George had cancelled their plans. They could've driven up the bay side of the Door County peninsula with its curving roads and scenic overlooks and made a stop at Al Johnson's for Swedish pancakes topped with lingonberries and whipped cream. Betsy's mouth watered just thinking about them.

Chloe turned onto their road and gasped.

"What's wrong?" Betsy whipped around to face her.

Chloe had stopped the car and was pointing at the house next door. "My neighbor's curtains are pulled back."

"Oh. That's...sort of interesting."

"How have I not talked to you about this?"

"I'm not sure." What was going on here? The little blue-gray Cape Cod, which was a nearly identical twin to Chloe's white one, was tranquil and ordinary. The curtains were drawn in the dormer windows upstairs like usual, but the view into the house was indeed unimpeded by the curtains in the downstairs windows.

"He's opened the windows, too," said Chloe.

"It does look that way."

"How do you not see what a big deal this is?"

"I'm confused."

"How have we not talked about this? Think about it. Have you ever seen my neighbor since he moved here in February?"

Betsy considered the question. "No," she said. "I haven't seen him at all." That was kind of odd, but maybe he just kept to himself.

"I haven't either." Chloe rolled Old Blue into the driveway and parked in her garage. "Well, almost never. I only had one glimpse, and that was when he was moving in. I've never even seen him outside to get his mail, and someone else came over to shovel the snow this winter. Also, he's got his lights on all night. I can see them through the cracks in the curtains sometimes." She was clearly struggling to contain herself.

"Is life getting a little tame for you these days?"

"What do you mean? This is fascinating." Betsy shrugged and Chloe's jaw dropped. "Where's your sense of adventure? I can't believe you aren't even a little curious about what's going on with this guy."

"What are the options? He's probably shy, or not interested in getting to know the neighbors."

"Or maybe..." Betsy could see Chloe's wheels turning as she spoke. "Maybe he's a bank robber. He's on the run from the law, and his face is plastered on those wanted posters they hang up at the bank. He's hidden the goods, and he's lying low until the dust has settled." Betsy tried to interrupt, but Chloe carried on. "Or maybe he was witness to a murder, and they've arrested the wrong person. The person who really did it was his boss, and his boss knows that this guy knows he did it. He has to hide out here until the real killer is brought to justice."

"Or maybe he picked up on a weird vibe from his neighbor on the other side of the fence."

"Mr. Franklin? He seems pretty normal to me."

Betsy rolled her eyes. "I was talking about you."

"Me? I'm totally normal. Way more normal than Mr. Franklin."

"Clearly."

"Seriously. You need to help me figure out what's going on with him." Chloe hopped out of the truck. Betsy met her by the tailgate. "Please. It could be a matter of life and death."

"I can see you think that, but what are we going to do? Knock on his door and ask him if he's hiding from the law?"

"No. That would never work. He won't tell me what's really going on. Knocking on his door's a good idea though. I thought I'd tell him I was going to be out of town next week, and ask him if he would keep an eye on the house."

"To what end?"

"To see his face, find out if he has shifty eyes."

Oh boy. "Did you try looking up his name? You can probably discover a lot about him without knocking on his door."

"Yeah. I did."

"So?"

"His name's Noah. He moved here from Georgia. That's all I can tell. Otherwise, he's basically invisible."

"Huh. No online presence. You have a point. That is a little strange, but what difference does it make? You have a business and a hunky farmer to focus on. Leave your neighbor alone."

"That's easy for you to say. You have four houses acting as a buffer."

Betsy could see that Chloe wasn't going to let this go. "I'll help you."

"Thank you."

"But only if you promise not to go overboard with this."

"Define overboard." Chloe opened the door. Marshmallow bolted out and did zoomies back and forth in the backyard.

"Nothing illegal. No peeking in his windows or breaking into his house."

"Look at us. You're the one warning *me* to keep it in line. A lot can change in a year."

Betsy couldn't argue with her about that. A whole lot had changed, and her baby wasn't even born yet. "I don't hear you promising." Betsy followed Chloe inside, where an explosion of papers had proliferated, spreading from the kitchen table to the coffee table overnight.

"I promise not to go overboard. I know it's probably silly, but I have a feeling something's up, and it's going to drive me crazy until I figure out what it is."

Chapter Six

In Which a Brother Hints at a Long-Buried Secret

"You didn't have to do that." Karl's mom opened the front door and took two bags of groceries out of his hands.

"I know." Karl stepped inside and slid off his shoes. "But I wanted to. I heard you were busy, and I was just sitting around at home. Might as well make myself useful."

"Nick told you we were running low, no doubt. You boys don't have to worry about us." She carried the groceries into the kitchen, set them on the table, and started to stash them away. "I sure do appreciate this. I would've gotten dressed if I'd known you were coming. Look at me: ten o'clock and still in my pajamas."

"Late night?"

"Very. I stayed after my shift because one of the residents is nearing her final days. She was one of my favorites, such a sweet woman."

"I'm so sorry."

"It's alright. That's life for you, but she'll be missed."

"I'm sure she appreciated having you with her,

and you look beautiful. Here, let me help you with that."

She swatted his hand away. "You just sit there and let me get you a cup of coffee." Karl reluctantly sat down at the table, and she handed him a steaming mug. "Did you eat breakfast yet?"

Karl looked past his mom into the nearly empty cupboards. "I ate right before I came over." His stomach grumbled at the thought of food; he covered it with a cough. He'd eat when he got home. He glanced into the living room. The old floral couch that had been there since he was a kid was just out of sight, but he could hear the intro music for his parents' favorite Sunday morning news show playing quietly on their little TV. "Where's Dad?"

"He's in there. He just woke up." She lowered her voice. "He's been sleeping in more often lately. I've been trying to talk him into taking up a new hobby, something he can get excited about, but I don't want to nag."

"Is he getting out at all?"

"Not much." Karl took that to mean not at all. "It'll cheer him up to see you. He's over the moon about Nick. It's all he talks about lately."

Karl nodded, took a sip of his scalding hot coffee, and carried it into the living room. His dad sat by the sliding glass door, watching finches visiting the bird feeder with a somber expression on his face. He had more stubble on his chin than usual, and the little bit of red hair he had on the top of his head stuck every which way.

"Hey, Dad."

His dad turned in surprise. "I didn't hear you come in. Did you just get here?"

"Yeah. I was in the kitchen with Mom. How's it going around here?" The house looked clean at least. There were vacuum lines in the mottled brown carpet. Nick, the neat nut in the family, had undoubtedly been up and cleaning before he left to volunteer at the nursing home this morning.

"Oh. You know how it is. It's been kind of quiet. The weather's getting nicer though."

"Maybe you and I could take a drive today."

"Maybe," his dad said, but Karl knew he wouldn't take him up on it.

Karl sat down and his dad rolled over to meet him. He pushed himself up and out of his wheel chair and onto the couch beside his son.

Karl plucked a newspaper out from between the lumpy cushions. "Look, it says the cherry blossoms are in full bloom this weekend. Are you sure I can't interest you in a ride?"

"Not today. I've got a full day ahead of me. Gotta conserve my energy."

"I understand. The offer's always on the table though." What else might work? "We could go out and shoot some hoops."

"Maybe later." His dad patted him on the leg. "You're a good son. How are things going at work? Your mom has people coming up to her all the time saying what a skilled mechanic you are and what a nice man we've raised. We're really proud of you."

Karl was taken aback. He tried to do a good job; he knew his way around the shop, but he didn't consider what he did anything special. "Thanks. That's nice to hear. It's going really well. There are a few puzzlers every week to keep me on my toes."

"You always were a smart one, like your brother." He shook his head. "Can't believe he's going to be a college man already. We finally got him there. Couldn't have done it without you."

"I don't know about that."

"I do."

"We did it together." His dad had fought his way back from losing the use of both his legs and debilitating depression. All Karl had done was throw together some meals and keep an eye on his brother.

Just then, Nick walked into the room. "Back already?" his dad asked.

"I'd been there since seven. It seems like I was never gone because you just woke up." Nick sat down on the other side of his dad and gave him a nudge.

"You've got a point there. We were just talking about you and your big plans."

Nick chuckled. "I'm not even certain exactly what they are yet." He turned to Karl. "Do you want to check out my room? I'm getting some stuff together, and I wanted your opinion."

"I'm not sure how much help I'll be. You need anything?" Karl asked his dad.

"I'm fine. You two go ahead." So Karl followed Nick upstairs and into his room. Nick closed the door behind them.

"What did you want to ask me about?" Karl sat down on Nick's perfectly smooth comforter while picturing his own messy unmade bed back at home. Along Nick's wall was a bookshelf stuffed to the brim with treasured finds collected from rummage sales or given as gifts for Christmases and birthdays. Nick always asked for books above anything else. Atop the bookshelf were trophies from science fairs and forensics competitions.

"It's not really about getting ready for college." Nick hesitated. "Well, it is, but not like that."

"What's up?"

"I'm starting to think it's not the best idea for me to go to school so far away. I could live at home, commute to Green Bay or Sturgeon Bay, something like that."

"But you always wanted to go to Madison. Is there some reason you've changed your mind other than the cost? Because what we've figured out should work." It would work as long as Karl still had a job come tomorrow morning, anyway. He didn't really have to ask his brother about his other concern. Nick's hesitation undoubtedly stemmed from the same reason Karl had never left Namur at all.

Nick turned his desk chair around to face his brother and plopped down. "Mom has so much to deal with, and Dad hasn't been doing well lately. I've been doing so much of the cooking and cleaning around here, and I worry about what will happen if I run off to pursue this selfish dream and leave them high and dry."

It was exactly as Karl had suspected. The guilt never really went away, the worry that you weren't doing enough, that it was selfish to move forward. Karl would've liked to have spared his younger brother the conflict that he himself wrestled with all the time, but ultimately he'd have to figure it out on his own.

"It's not like that," Karl said. "We all want this for you, and anyway, you deserve to do something for yourself. Mom and Dad will be fine. I'll be here. I can come over more often than I have been lately. I have work, but that's my only real responsibility. I can come over every day if they need me to."

Nick wasn't convinced. "If I stay at home and start out at the technical college, it'll save us so much money. I don't know if it's right to ask you to pay for me to go off to school when there's a perfectly good option close to home."

"I volunteered to do it. No one's pressuring me."

Nick picked up a completed Rubik's Cube and twisted it in his hands, jumbling the colors. "You didn't leave. You stayed here and helped out. Mom and Dad did all they could, but I was only five when he got hurt. I remember you making dinner most nights, and you were the one who always checked my homework. You were doing more of the parenting than they were a lot of the time."

"And I didn't do all that work to have you give up on what you want." Karl was more frustrated than he was letting on. It wasn't as if he didn't understand where Nick was coming from. Karl had been in a similar position and had to make the decision that was right at the time, but this was a different time and a completely different circumstance. They'd both come a long way since then.

Nick nodded, setting the cube back on his desk. "I want to be sure I'm doing the right thing."

"You are. Your going to college was one of the first things Dad brought up when I walked into the room. Besides, it's only four years, and you can come back every summer if you want to."

Nick looked away. "I feel like I'm abandoning them."

"You're not. We'll all be mad at you if you don't go when you really wanted to. If you decide to do something else, that's great. You're going to be a success no matter what you choose. We'll support you either way, but don't stay on my account or theirs. That's not what any of us want."

"I don't know. I appreciate you saying that, but it doesn't make me feel less uncomfortable about it."

"Can you imagine what it'll mean to Dad to see you walking across the stage at your college graduation? That's your dream. It's his too."

"Okay. I'll stay the course for now. I can always try it for a year and do something else if it doesn't work out, but you have to promise to keep me posted on how things are going over here. No keeping stuff from me so I don't worry."

"I'll be in touch. I promise."

"And another thing-while we're talking about

being honest-what's going on with you and Betsy?"

Karl cocked his head, confused. "Why do you keep asking me about this all of a sudden?"

"Because it's not just Mom and Dad I'm worried about. If I'm going to be leaving, I'd also feel better if you were happy here."

"What do you mean? I am happy."

"I know you're satisfied, but I mean *happy*. Like, really happy. The last time I saw you and Betsy together, I could tell something was up. You're always smiling when you're with her."

"Are you talking about when she stopped over Friday night? She wanted me check something out on her car."

"That's what you said, but she was looking at you like you were an ice cream sundae."

"No, she wasn't. I think I would've noticed that."

"Would you have?"

"Ummm...yes."

"She was blushing and looking up at your through her eyelashes like a Disney princess."

"She told me her face had been turning red because she's pregnant. I know you love her, and you've always been rooting for us, but I tried. She's not interested in me."

"When did you try?" Nick asked with skepticism.

"I don't know...in high school I guess. I asked her to a dance. She didn't realize it was a date, though. She ended up making out with some other guy at the end of the night."

"Ouch."

"Yeah. She did apologize for leaving me, but she said she knew I'd understand since we were 'such good friends'."

"But you were what, sixteen then?"

"And what's changed? She's with George and pregnant with his baby. From what I've seen, he's a truly terrible boyfriend, but what can I do? I've been cast as the platonic friend."

"I'm telling you, that's not how it looked the other night."

"I'm not getting my hopes up, not anymore. I'm working on getting over her. I've been working on it." Hearing that she was gazing at him adoringly, even if Nick was wrong, wasn't helping. "Given George's dependability, I get the feeling she's going to need a friend more than anything, not some poor schmuck who's still in love with her."

"See? You admit it. You're in love with her. It's like I'm always telling you, you're too nice. I get where you're coming from, though. She was there for us when we were having a rough time. Remember how she'd take me out to Emma's and they'd pretend it was my birthday every other week? Six-year-old me thought that was so cool."

Karl did remember. Betsy, the youngest in a family of three sisters, took Nick under her wing as the little brother she'd never had. She carted him around to baseball practice when no one else could take him and stayed to cheer him on. She took him to the beach, too. Nick would return home coated with sticky white sand, full of stories about the moat they'd dug around their sandcastle, or how Betsy had let him bury her up to her neck.

She'd been a great friend. Karl wanted more for her than what George had to offer, but that was up to her. Karl would be the one cheering her on from the sidelines, regardless of how she managed her love life.

"Weren't you and George friends for a while?" Nick asked. "I thought he came over sometimes in the summer when he was back from college."

"No. We were never friends."

"Huh. I must've imagined it."

Nick was partly right, though. As much as Karl tried to forget it, George had stopped over every now and then the summer Karl turned eighteen, but he and George were never friends, and they never would be. Karl could barely tolerate him as an acquaintance. He knew far too much about the kind of man George had been and undoubtedly still was.

Chapter Seven

In Which Wes Makes a Naked Confession of His Own

"Can you wipe down these teats for me?" Bea washed her hands at the metal sink in the corner of the barn.

"I thought you'd never ask," Wes said, coming up behind her and wrapping his arms around her waist.

She flicked him with a towel. "Very funny. Vincent van Goat gets impatient on her platform, and I don't want her trying to step off."

Wes proudly washed the goats' teats in a Dawn Dish Soap solution and dried them off with a paper towel, giving a little extra flourish at the end. He couldn't believe he was now an expert at milking goats. It wasn't a life mission that had been on his radar prior to reuniting with Bea last year, but once he honed in on his goal, he was determined to see it through.

He was a little offended that Vincent van Goat didn't seem to be overly fond of him. "Sorry about the name," he said as he attended to her. "I didn't know how to tell a girl goat from a boy goat when we first met. I thought you looked like a Vincent, but now you're coming into your own." She gave him a side eye and stomped her hoof. Oh well, he had plenty of time to win her over.

After hearing the names that Bea had picked out for her resident goats, Wes couldn't resist naming the newly born kids himself, with input from her niece and nephew who lived across the street. There were still plenty of Stripes and Spotties running around, but they were now joined by Billy the Kid, Goatzilla, and Billy Nye the Goat Guy.

Bea followed behind him, hooking each goat up to the milking machine. "Thanks for staying over the other night, or yesterday, or whatever you would call it. I couldn't believe it when you walked through the door."

"I'm glad I happened to be passing by. It's not often I'm out all night."

"Right? What were the chances?" Bea wiped her forehead with the back of her arm. The morning was heating up already.

"You can call me any time, day or night, if you need help."

"Thanks. I know. That's really sweet of you, but one of us should get some sleep."

Wes sat down on one of the low stools in the corner of the milking area while Bea walked around to each goat, ensuring that they were all comfortable. They chomped at their feed, watching her as she passed.

"I want to be here for you. I'm only down the

road, and pretty soon I'll be here all the time. Are you sure you're ready for that?" he teased.

"I'm more worried about you being ready for all this." Bea sat down on the stool next to him.

He waved her concern away, but he'd been thinking the same thing. If he was uneasy about the responsibility of offering advice to troubled villagers, that was nothing compared to how he felt about being jointly responsible for a whole farm and two elderly parents.

"I'm ready," he said. "I can't wait to marry you." That last part was true. Wes and Bea had dated all through high school, only to break up over a decade ago, when her dad encouraged her to end her relationship with the goofy guy with the overactive imagination. Thankfully, her dad had come around last year when he saw how happy they were together, but Wes had a sinking feeling that he may have been partially right. What if Bea would've been better off with a strapping local farmer, as opposed to a clumsy librarian who couldn't tell a girl goat from a boy?

As the goats' milk slowed in its path through the tube, Bea got up to unhook the machine and let the goats loose into the bigger enclosure. "I can't wait to get married either. It won't be much longer now. It almost doesn't seem real. I was over at Lindsay's barn yesterday morning, and it really hit me that this was where we'd be having our reception. It's decorated to look like a circus tent now, but I let Lindsay know that we'd be taking our event in a different direction."

"Without consulting me?" Wes asked. "I was

hoping to do face painting and balloon animals."

"Ooh. That's actually a really good idea."

"It is? I was kidding."

"I know. I meant for the Demeter Society fundraising fair. I'll suggest that to Lindsay when I see her next. Can you really make balloon animals?"

"I really can."

"Why didn't I know that about you?"

"I guess it never came up."

"Wait...why do you know how to make balloon animals? You couldn't do that as a kid, which means you picked it up in your adult life for some reason."

Wes got up and stretched his arms over his head. "It's a long story. Want to head outside?"

Bea did. They left the barn and strolled across the yard to the picnic table, which sat beneath a fragrant flowering peach tree. The sun beat down on their backs as they sat side by side. Bea rested her head on Wes's shoulder. He smoothed her hair from her brow and kissed her forehead. When they were alone like this, everything felt so simple.

"So you want to know how I learned to create balloon animals...this story is nestled into another story, which is kind of embarrassing. Are you sure you want to hear the whole thing?"

Bea sat up at attention and grinned. "Of course I do, especially when you put it like that. Here I was, thinking we knew everything there was to know about each other, and you have all these fun secrets."

"I don't know if 'fun' is the right word...is there

anything I don't know about you?"

"Hmm. Probably. I'll think about it while you tell me your story."

"Like so many great tales," Wes began, "this one starts with the World Naked Bike Ride. I trust you're familiar with the event?"

Bea laughed. "Not at all."

"I didn't really think you would be. It's a big deal in some cities. I think the biggest one's in Portland."

"Is it exactly what it sounds like?"

"Pretty much. People ride their bikes, naked, in a big group on a route. It's like any other bike race, but instead of spandex, people wear nothing-maybe a tutu if they're feeling modest. So anyway, they held one in Madison two years ago, and Hugh insisted that I do it with him. It's a protest against consumerism and our national dependence on fossil fuels, and you know how passionate Hugh is about...well, everything.

"At first I was dead set against it, but then Hugh showed me a video of the ride in Portland, and there were all these thousands of people there. It was a big party atmosphere, and I thought it might actually be kind of fun. I'd done a bunch of bike races before, and it looked like it would be just like that, except more leisurely and without clothes."

"I still don't understand how balloon animals factor in," said Bea. Wes could tell she was getting a kick out of this story, and that was a good sign. He could've seen her being appalled, but then again, she knew who she'd gotten involved with and was choosing to marry him anyway.

"Hugh suggested we could make balloon animal crowns and hand them out before the race. I found a book all about it, one thing led to another, and I got a little carried away. Pretty soon I could make poodles and swords. The swords were the most popular sculpture at the race. And that's how I learned to make balloon animals. I'm a little rusty, but I could pick it up pretty quick."

"That's it?" Bea asked.

"That's how I learned to make balloon animals."

"You know that's not what I mean. You're not going to tell me how the race went?"

Wes glanced away with a grimace. "Other than the fun of making the balloon animals, it was kind of awful. It turns out, instead of the thousands I'd seen in Portland, there were about forty people doing it in Madison, mostly guys, and most of our spectators didn't know what was going on. Apparently, Wisconsin was unprepared for that kind of weirdness. A woman shrieked and covered her children's faces when we came by. We had a permit and everything, but we probably seemed like a deranged group of deviants to most of the outside world."

"Huh."

"Is that a good huh or a bad huh?"

"It's neither. I love your sense of adventure, but that's pretty wild."

Now it was Wes's turn to laugh. "What about

you?"

"I think I'll pass on the naked bike festival."

"I was wondering if there's anything about you that would surprise me, but it's good to know where you stand on that. I was hoping to make it a family tradition."

"Sorry. I haven't met our particular kids yet, but I'm pretty sure kids are universally appalled by the idea of their parents running around naked in public."

"Darn. I need to read more parenting books."

Bea pursed her lips and turned serious. Had she thought of something important? "Okay. I've thought of my thing."

"It sounds big."

"It is. This is a family-wide secret, and it's bizarre. I've never told you about it, because none of us talk about it. Starting after I tell you, you're not allowed to say a word about it either."

"Can I decide after you tell me?"

"Nope. You have to promise you won't repeat this." Wes promised, figuring if it was something really strange, he could break his oath. He wouldn't have thought it was anything crazy before his stint as a mobile librarian, but he was now wise to the truth about what strange issues were lurking beneath the surface of the placid waters of this village.

Bea scanned the farmyard, checking if the coast was clear, before she said, "There's this magnet. It's a green M&M. You know- the girl one, with the white boots and the long eyelashes."

"I'm scared."

"You should be," Bea said. "This is scary stuff. Are you sure you want me to go on?"

Wes nodded, but he wasn't totally certain.

"So this magnet, I'm not sure where it came from, but I can't remember a time when it wasn't in the house." Bea looked at Wes as if she expected a reaction, but he was just confused. "It shows up everywhere, and whenever I find it, I move it somewhere else, but it never stays there for long."

"And this has been going on for..."

"Since Harvey and I were kids."

"And no one ever talks about it."

"No. That's what makes it so funny. We're all in on it, but no one ever mentions a thing."

"Why is this the first I'm hearing about this?"

"Because you're going to live here. What if you found her on top of the toilet and you spoke up?"

"That would be...bad?"

"Yes! You'd break the spell."

Huh. Wes never would've guessed that a secret magnet game was going on right under his nose. "I feel privileged to be let in on this, but also relieved that I never ran into her at your house and asked what was up with the roving M&M."

"There have been a couple of close calls, but I sneaked her out of the way before you could spot her."

"See? This is what I love about you guys."

"That we have a wandering magnet that we must never speak of starting now?"

"Yes, but not only that. Growing up, it was just

me and my mom, for the most part. I love her, but she's so artsy and out there; we didn't do typical stuff. You have all these great family traditions. You live in the house your great-grandparents built. You bake recipes that are a hundred years old. Your parents have been together forever, and your brother lives across the street with his kids: one boy and one girl. It's all so...so perfect and together. Sorry, I'm not making any sense."

"No. You are. I appreciate you saying that, because I don't want to take what we have here for granted. Lately I've had a tendency to focus on the things we're struggling with as a family."

Wes pulled Bea in for a hug, and she rested her head on his chest. "Is there anything else I don't know about you?" she asked. "Any naked triathlons or nude mini-golf competitions?"

Wes thought about it. He was terrified of messing up what she had going on with this beautiful farm that had been in her family for generations. He really did admire it all, but what did he know about being a farmer? The stone summer kitchen stood, solid and cool, behind the red brick farmhouse. Bea's garden, her expansive fields, and her classic barn looked like something out of a magazine. So did Bea, for that matter, with her sweet round face, rose patterned barn boots, and her flannel shirt, rolled up to the elbows. Up until his wedding, the only places Wes would have lived were his Mom's house, rented apartments, and his current residence: a cabin by a pond, both of which belonged to his uncle.

He'd never even had a pet, not so much as a goldfish. Cedar Hollow Farm was crawling with animals. There were the goats, of course, but there were also chickens and cats galore. As if on cue, a sleek black tomcat prowled past them, intent on something they couldn't see in last year's matted grass along the fence line.

No, Bea couldn't know that he was getting nervous about handling all this responsibility. There was no way, none that he could think of anyway, that he could tell her about his trepidation without sounding like he wasn't thrilled about the prospect of spending the rest of their lives together. And the thing was, he really was thrilled. Thrilled and terrified, both. He wanted to be a man who could confidently take this all on, but was he?

"Nope. No more surprises from me," he said.

"Me either," said Bea, tilting her chin up to kiss him.

Wes would jump in feet first. He could do this, and he would. If only he could get past his jangling nerves enough to feel the confidence he so desperately needed.

Chapter Eight

In Which a Time Traveler Reaches Out

Outside the nursery window, a rain so light it was barely there fell from a steel gray sky. It clung to the windows in tiny spots until enough water collected for a single large drop to slide down, snake-like, in a meandering path to the windowsill.

Inside the house it was far more cheery. Bunny pictures, gifted by Chloe, hung over the crib on a powder pink wall, while a fluttery iridescent butterfly mobile dangled from the ceiling. A chair in the corner would serve as the perfect nursing station. Betsy leaned over her belly to pick tiny cotton onesies out of the laundry basket. She folded them on a pink and white striped ottoman then secreted them away in the dresser.

Much like her pregnancy, the spare room had taken shape little by little until Betsy thought of it as the official nursery. She pictured her little girl asleep in the crib or crawling across the soft gray and white scalloped rug, and her heart was full.

There was really very little left to do to get ready. The diapers and wipes were stacked beneath the changing table. The crib had been difficult for

Betsy to assemble until Chloe took over, making it look like she could've done the job one-handed. A soft yellow blanket, knitted by Sarah, draped over the bars of the crib, ready and waiting to wrap up a sweet little newborn.

It was about time that newborn had a name, but Betsy hadn't come across one that fit yet. When she found the right one, she knew it would feel exactly right. She'd scoured the internet for names that were unique, ones she wouldn't have thought of off the top of her head, but nothing stood out to her as being the name her daughter should have for the rest of her life.

Betsy looked out the window at the rain-washed street. Chloe would have been working for at least an hour by now. Betsy should head over there. Lately, she felt overheated all the time. It would be refreshing to stroll the short distance between their houses in the cool drizzle. She reluctantly left the room, closing the door behind her.

By the time she stood outside on the sidewalk, the rain had stopped. Betsy folded up her umbrella. Unseen birds twittered to each other from her neighbor's backyard and a dog, probably Marshmallow, sent out a couple of deep barks from down the road.

Betsy slowed as she neared the little gray Cape Cod next to Chloe's house. Had she seen a curtain twitch? She stopped. The curtains in the downstairs windows, which were closed again, were still. Chloe's theories about the mystery neighbor must've been getting to her.

Not wanting to stand there staring, Betsy continued on her way until she'd reached Chloe's back door. She let herself in. As expected, Chloe was at the kitchen table, her eyes squinting at the computer in front of her. Marshmallow reclined in her favorite cushy bed.

Chloe didn't look up as she asked, "Can you grab my coffee? I'm right in the middle of having a great idea, and I don't want to move."

Betsy picked up the half full mug of coffee next to the sink. Nearly room temperature, a skim of grease coiled along its surface. "Do you want me to warm this up?"

Chloe held up one finger and carried on typing away, pausing to take notes on a paper pad. She stabbed the paper with her pen. "That's it!" she yelled. "Ha!"

She stood up and rubbed her eyes. "Sorry, I got an idea at four this morning, and I've been working on it ever since."

Betsy knew not to ask what the idea was. Chloe would only tell her when she was sure she could make it happen, and she would reveal it in the most dramatic fashion possible.

Chloe grabbed the mug out of Betsy's hand and took a generous gulp. "Did you pass *the house* on the way here?"

"Which house?" Betsy asked, knowing full well which house Chloe was referring to.

"The one with the creepy neighbor."

"Are you asking if I took the only possible

route from my house to yours without flying?"

Chloe poured herself another cup of coffee and drank half of it before answering. "Well, I know you passed it, but was there anything strange about it?"

Should she tell Chloe she thought she'd seen the curtains twitch? It might have been her eyes playing tricks on her, and who knew how far Chloe would go if she got seriously curious about the invisible man. On the other hand, Chloe was having fun with it, and as her life had been revolving around work more often than not lately, she could use a diversion. Betsy would tell her. If Chloe was looking for a mystery, a mystery is what she'd get. "I'm not positive about this, so don't freak out."

Chloe spit her coffee back into the mug. "You did see something?"

"You're freaking out already, and I haven't even told you."

"I'm as calm as can be." The coffee in her cup jiggled along with her trembling hand.

Betsy sighed. Maybe this had been a bad idea, but she'd already admitted there had been something, and it was such a little thing. "I'm not even positive that I really saw it. The curtains might have twitched as I got close to the house."

Chloe dropped her mug on the counter. "I knew it! Someone's in there, and he's watching us. That's it…it's time for action."

A twitching curtain was a call to action?

"What are you going to do?" Betsy asked.

Chloe sat back down at the table, leaving her

coffee to get cold again. She always drank exactly half then let the other half get cold. "I'm following through with my plan to knock on the door and tell him I'll be out of town next week. Or...maybe that's a bad idea. If I do that, I'll have to hide out when I said I'd be gone. I could work from Arthur's farm, but I need access to my workshop. Okay, scratch that."

"Done."

"You're not taking this seriously enough, but that's fine. You'll be thanking me when I save the neighborhood, maybe even the whole town. Okay, the out of town idea's out. What if I bring him some muffins?" Chloe leapt up, strode across the room, fumbled around in the drawer beneath her oven, and pulled out two seldom-used muffin pans. "I'll say I meant to welcome him to the neighborhood, but I'd been busy and hadn't had the chance until today."

Betsy cleared a space at the table and fired up her laptop. "Do you want me to help? Otherwise, I'm going to start sorting through e-mails. You know how swamped I get on Mondays."

Chloe barely acknowledged her as she lugged a bulky unopened bag of flour off the top shelf of her pantry. "Yeah. Do what you have to, but I'm going to need you to be lurking the shadows when I knock on the door."

"Whatever you say, boss."

The e-mails were a mix of the usual things: questions about their products, a request to do a podcast, statements from a couple of other businesses, and...yes! A review from Gadgetgal.

Between replying to a slew of questions and supervising Chloe's mission, it was going to be a full day. Why not check out a gag review to start out on the right foot? "I got another funny one," Betsy called over to Chloe.

"Ooh. Read it out loud." Chloe dumped a deluge of frozen blueberries into the muffin batter, which she had somehow managed to mix up in two point two seconds. She wasn't kidding when she said she wanted to discover her mystery man's identity.

With my (human) boyfriend out of the way, I've found fresh inspiration to dedicate my life to a passion I'd been putting off for years: time travelling zoology. Upon embarking on my first journey, I discovered a troubling roadblock: none of my tools were effectively traversing the space-time continuum in one piece. They'd dissolve into a thousand shiny sparkles upon arrival. I was about to give up hope of ever being able to haul a wooly mammoth baby or dinosaur egg back to the present, when I inadvertently discovered that Dirk (aka shovel boyfriend) successfully made the journey without my knowledge. (I never would have consented to allowing him to risk his life for my project, but he sneaked into the time machine.) Would it work with your other tools? Eureka! It did. One wheelbarrow, an inattentive trilobite mother, and the manual dexterity of a cheetah later, and I had myself an extinct marine artiopodan arthropod. Thanks Bare Roots Tools!

"Pretty sure that one's my favorite," said Chloe as she slid her muffins into the oven.

"Personally, I liked the one where she fell for

Dirk. Who do you think this is? I bet I can figure it out before you can."

Chloe chugged her cooled coffee and sat down. "Ooh. Is this a real bet? Because there's no way you could best me when it comes to a game of secret identities."

"Of course it is."

"Got it." Chloe flipped a page in her notepad, poised to create a record of their wagers. "What are the stakes?"

Betsy considered. "The loser has to make dinner and dessert for a week."

"And we can find out who it is by any means necessary?"

"Is there any other way?" Betsy didn't wait for an answer. "Should I reply?"

"You haven't replied yet? What did I hire you for?"

"To craft funny responses to joke e-mails?"

"Precisely. Now get to work. Do you need any help?"

"Hmm...I'll let you know if I get stuck, but I have some good ideas."

Both women typed away while the smell of blueberry muffins gradually filled the kitchen. Betsy chuckled to herself while Chloe went back to stabbing her notepaper with a pen and punching calculations into a spreadsheet.

Dear Satisfied Customer, Betsy began. *Thank you for your helpful feedback on our world-class ergonomic tools for women like you, and congratulations on finding love. Our business was conceived through our own humble beginnings as time traveling climatologists. It thrills us to hear that you've discovered their secret properties as well as their more common uses. We're a little concerned though. Did you steal our time machine prototype or develop yours independently? Be warned, ours stopped reliably returning after the 15th use. Not sure where (or when, hehe) one of our associates ended up being stranded.*

Best wishes, Betsy

Customer Service Representative, Bare Roots Tools

"Do you want to read it before I send it off?"

Chloe didn't look up from her calculating. "Nah. Working. Can't stop." She banged herself over the head with the notepad and went back to typing.

Betsy hit send and moved along to more serious business like....

Beep Beep Beep

"The muffins are ready." Chloe hopped up from her chair. "Now go change into some black clothes so you can blend in with the shadows."

Chloe yanked the muffins onto a couple of waiting hot pads and flicked them out of the tin with a fork.

"Are you joking?" Betsy asked.

"Do I look like I'm joking?" The ink from Chloe's notebook had transferred to her forehead.

"Yes. And doesn't it make more sense to wear black at night? I'll probably stand out more if I'm hiding behind a tree dressed all in black." Outside the window, Chloe's neatly mowed yard and newly planted garden basked in the sunshine. It wouldn't be difficult to see someone dressed as a ninja out there. "Why don't I watch you out the window? I'll have my phone in my hand. If he yanks you into the house or starts throwing garbage at you, I'll be on the phone with backup in seconds."

Chloe took a deep breath and puffed it out. It took a while for her to come to terms with a change in plans, but she usually came around eventually. "Okay. You can stay in the safety of the house. Release the hound if I give you the signal." Betsy didn't bother asking what the signal was. Marshmallow certainly was a big dog, but that was about all she had going for her as a source of protection. "There's a front and back exit if you need to use either one. Unless there are two of them..."

"What do you think is realistically going to happen here? The most likely scenario is that he's a normal person who works nights, and you're going to wake him up."

"You're probably right, but that doesn't mean we shouldn't prepare for any eventuality."

"Do you have sharp cheddar?"

"Why do I need sharp cheddar?" Chloe looked panicky, and Betsy was almost sorry about teasing her. Almost, but not quite, because her sister was being ridiculous.

"What if he opens the door with a plate full of crackers, and he's just run out of cheese. Would you be prepared for that, because if you're not-oh boy-will both of your faces be red."

"This is no laughing matter."

"I agree. I'm trying to look at this situation from every angle. Frankly, I'm a little disappointed you're not taking it more seriously."

Chloe sighed. "Fine. Make fun. I know it's silly, but the tension's been building ever since he moved in. I've never even seen him drive anywhere. He probably doesn't have a car. He's just in there...plotting."

And to think Betsy thought they were coming to a more rational place. Chloe picked up her plate of muffins and headed for the door. "How do I look?"

"You're still in your pajamas."

Chloe looked down, gasped, and pounded upstairs to get dressed.

"You're also going to want to look in the mirror," Betsy yelled up the stairs.

When Chloe returned five minutes later, her hair was braided, she had on daytime clothes, and the calculations were wiped off her forehead. "Here I go. Wish me luck."

"Go get em." Betsy walked Chloe to the door then manned her station at the side window. Chloe strolled down the street with the tray of muffins in her hands, whistling a tune that Betsy could just barely hear through the screen. She was so inconspicuous in her attempt to be inconspicuous that she might as well yell, "Nothing to see here."

She rapped at the front door, balancing the muffins with one hand. A moment later, it looked like she was having a conversation with someone. She even laughed. Huh. This was good. Chloe could finally put all this worry behind her.

She set the muffins on the porch and left, speed walking all the way home.

Betsy opened the door. "So, how did it go? It looked like it went well from here."

Chloe shook her head, her eyes wide. "No. It did not go well, not well at all. I didn't even get to see him."

"Who were you talking to?"

"The neighbor."

"But you didn't see him?"

"No. He talked to me through an intercom. He thought I was the grocery delivery people, and he asked me to leave them on the mat. When I told him I was his neighbor, he said, 'I don't have any neighbors.' I laughed a little, thinking he might be joking, but he didn't say anything else after that."

"What did he sound like?"

"He had a deep voice, kind of Eastern European sounding."

"Really? I know this is bugging you, but I think you should leave him alone now. It was nice of you to bring him muffins. I bet he'll appreciate them, but he obviously has something going on that's none of our business."

Chloe nodded. "I agree."

"You do?" Betsy hadn't expected it to be that easy.

"Yeah. I was really curious, but it looks like that'll be it. I was thinking," Chloe went on, "what if he's agoraphobic or something? I shouldn't harass him. Now that I've heard a voice and know there's a real person in there, I feel better. I was getting a bad feeling, and I've been trying to trust that, but enough is enough."

What a relief. Betsy had been steeling herself for a month at the least of being on high alert, but all it had taken to call Chloe off were some muffins and a knock on the door. Who would've guessed?

After all that excitement, the sisters worked straight through until lunch. Betsy was getting more proficient at answering calls and e-mails. All those years of being a waitress had made her a master of small talk and dealing with dissatisfied customers. Not that they had many of those. Most people just wanted to gush about how amazing their products were or were calling to ask when they'd start making x, y, or z.

"Do you want to take a break for lunch?" Chloe asked.

"I'd love to. What did you have in mind?"

Chloe pulled out a plate of muffins. "They looked too good to give them all away."

Betsy took two and poured herself a glass of milk. "Hey," she said as she sat back down in front of her computer. "Another e-mail from Gadgetgal."

Hi Betsy, Glad to hear we're in a similar field, but sorry about your colleague. If I ever bump into her, I'll bring her back. To clarify, I'm not a woman. Gadgetguy was taken, so I got the next best thing. I developed my own time machine in the future but enjoyed this decade so much that I decided to stick around. No doubt you and Chloe have already started betting on who I am, so I'll give you a clue: I'm not the first person you think of.

Chloe, who had been reading over her shoulder asked, "Who did you think of first?"

"Who did you?"

"Let's say it at the same time."

"Wes," they both said.

"This is so his sense of humor," said Chloe. "Can't you just see him chuckling to himself in the bookmobile?"

"I can, but how would he know that we'd think of him first?"

"I'm not sure. This is a puzzler. I'm planning on going over there tonight. I'll mention the emails and see if I get a reaction."

"Will you tell me what he says?"

Chloe looked scandalized. "No way. You're the competition."

"If that's how you want to play it."

"I do."

They got back to work. After a long day and an excellent dinner, Chloe drove over to the mobile library before it closed, and Betsy walked home. She passed the little gray house. The muffins were gone, likely taken inside. She hoped the man who lived there was alright. He probably worked from home and liked his privacy. It was wise of Chloe to let him be. The e-mail mystery would be their side project now. Betsy loved a good sister competition. Now if only she could figure out who was sending those e-mails.

Chapter Nine

In Which Karl Receives the Offer of a Lifetime

Earlier that day, Karl walked into the shop to find Frank waiting for him at the front desk. "Mornin'," said Frank, the computer screen reflected in his glasses.

"Hey," said Karl. That was always the extent of their morning greeting.

Determined not to be the one to bring up Friday's text, Karl grabbed a set of keys in the drop box and pulled a Ford F-150 into the shop. Jumping out of the truck, he strode over to the vintage tractor calendar on the side wall. Karl flipped the calendar from May to June. It was June 1st. What would happen if he got fired today? Nick started school at the end of August. If Karl started looking now, that would give him less than three months to find another job that paid as well as this one.

Frank was surly, but he appreciated a good mechanic. He paid better than anyone else for miles around. Karl would undoubtedly have to commute to find a better paying job, and that would add to his expenses. As it stood now, the shop was so close to his house that he could walk there most days when the weather was decent.

He headed back to the truck, determined to keep his mind on his work. The wrench he'd grabbed from the rack felt slippery in his sweaty hands as he popped the hood of the truck. What was going on under here? He'd talked to Arthur about taking it easier on this thing, but he still insisted on driving through giant puddles and across rutted logging roads at full speed.

Frank pulled another truck into the stall next to him and slid out, slamming the door behind him. He walked over to Karl, watching him work. This was different. What was Frank up to? Karl would keep on working like he always did. No need to force the issue.

Frank rocked back on his heels and nodded his head: sure signs he was about to say something of significance. "Yup. Saw you got my text."

Karl kept his face bland and his voice casual. "I did."

"Said I wanted to talk about something."

Karl nodded back in acknowledgement.

"Well," Frank went on, "I've been thinking about retiring."

Oh. This was news to Karl. Frank couldn't have been much past his mid-fifties.

"I'm ready to take it easier, ya know? I'm coming home sore from leaning over these grills all day," he smacked the side of the truck, "and then waking up even sorer. Never used to feel it when I was a young guy like you, but doing it full-time at my age? It's taking its toll."

Did this mean Frank was going to sell the shop?

Would the next owner want to keep Karl on? Frank would give him a glowing reference-well, not glowing, nothing Frank did could be said to glow-but a positive one nonetheless. Sometimes people had their own ideas about who they wanted to work with though, and Karl might not fit into the next owner's plans.

"So...I have a proposition for you," said Frank.

Karl turned his attention away from the truck and onto his boss.

Frank didn't make eye contact. Instead he scanned the room, looking anywhere but directly at Karl. "I'd like to sell you the shop. I'll stay on part-time a couple days a week."

What? Was he serious? "Wow. I don't know what to say. This is a huge opportunity for me, and I would be thrilled to own the shop but..."

"You're wondering how you'll be able to buy me out?"

"Right."

"You can do it over time, gradually. I'd like to see you running this place. I didn't build it from the ground up just to sell it to some yayhoo who'll do a shoddy job and overcharge people."

"I don't know..."

"Yeah, ya do. You work hard and you're good, better than me, but you'll never hear me admit that again. I don't like most people. I like you. I'll give you the place for a steal, and you'll make more as the owner. Unless you have some other reason not to agree to my offer that's better than being nervous about taking the risk, I'm not taking no for an answer."

Karl took a deep breath. Frank was right. There was no good reason for him not to jump at this chance. And he *was* afraid. He'd seen how life could knock you down when you least expected it, and he wasn't one to take any chances. What was the downside of this, though? It was arguably riskier to be the shop's owner, but it had been thriving in this town for thirty years.

"You're right. I'd be out of my mind not to accept. You have no idea how much..."

"Yup," Frank interrupted, sidestepping out the door that led back into the office. "I think we've said what we need to say here. I need to work some things out on my end, but I'll be in touch in the next couple of days about the details." He was about to leave the room when he added, "Don't breathe a word about this to anyone. I haven't even told my family yet. The prospect of me lurking around the house more often is going to send my wife into a fit."

"Of course. I won't say anything. It'll take me a while to process this anyway. Thank you. It's such a big..."

"Yup. I'll be in touch." Frank went back into the office, where he'd likely stay for the rest of the morning.

The office tended to be busy on Monday mornings, but Karl also suspected that Frank would be steering clear for at least a couple of days in order to avoid witnessing any further displays of emotion.

Karl would try to keep it together, but this was huge. He desperately wanted to tell someone, but he had no choice but to hold off. Just wait until his parents and Nick heard about this. It would be a big responsibility, but it was also a fantastic opportunity.

Maybe his luck was finally turning around.

Karl had a few easy jobs in the morning. He checked his phone over his lunch break in the afternoon. Betsy would be in tonight with her car. He was looking forward to seeing her even more than usual. He shook his head to clear the vivid image of her in her waitressing apron from his mind. He needed to cut this out. Nick's suggestion that she was interested in him was getting to him more than he cared to admit.

Maybe he'd meet someone nice when he did the bachelor auction at the end of the month. He couldn't believe he'd let Chloe talk him into it. He wouldn't have agreed to it at all if it wasn't for a good cause. Who else would be there? He knew everyone in town, but it sounded like Chloe was advertising as far north as Gill's Rock. If that was the case, there could be a horde of single women vying for a date with him. He hadn't been on a date in ages. Dating felt like so much work for what often ended up being very little reward.

It wasn't that Karl was picky. He wanted to be with someone he could have fun with but who also understood that his family came first. His last girlfriend seemed uncomfortable with his dad and uninterested in doing the kinds of things he enjoyed.

Simple things, like hiking or taking a picnic to the beach. She'd been relatively high maintenance too, not the right fit for a mechanic with basic tastes and a tight budget.

When his lunch break ended, Karl got back to work on an old Corvette. He immersed himself in the tasks of the day until 5:30, when Frank came in to say he was heading out. "You don't mind closing, do ya?" he asked.

"Not at all. I'm just finishing up." Karl wiped his hands with a greasy rag.

Frank grunted out, "Good. See ya tomorrow," and left Karl alone for another hour to wait for Betsy.

Karl carried on working. There was no reason not to use the time to catch up, and work would keep his mind off his beautiful friend and their secret rendezvous.

The hour flew by. Before Karl knew it, Betsy swept into the room in a long, tight maternity dress. It dipped in the front, with tiny pearlescent buttons down the neckline. Her thick blonde hair was piled on top of her head, exposing her long elegant neck.

Any concerns Karl had been mulling over in his mind disappeared at the sight of her.

Checking if the coast was clear, Betsy tiptoed over to him and squeezed his arm. His skin felt burning hot beneath her touch. He felt everything within him tense, as if waiting to spring. If only she could see what he was thinking right now...but she couldn't, and he'd never tell.

"So, what's next? Do you want me to pull my

car in?" she asked.

"What?"

"My car. Do you want to get it, or should I? I didn't want anything to look suspicious. Are you okay?"

"I'm fine," Karl said, snapping out of it. "You have a seat. Unless you're interested in helping me with the job...it appears you've come prepared." He tugged on a soft knotted gray band wrapped around her head.

"I'd be happy to assist, but it might be tricky for me to bend over enough to do much to help."

Betsy gently wiped a spot of something from his cheek. Had she always looked up at him through her eyelashes like that? What if Nick was right? No. Enough of this wishful thinking. Karl needed to get this job finished fast and move along before he made a fool of himself.

"You always get a little spot of grease there," she said, "right beneath your eye."

"It's messy work," he said quickly, "but I was teasing about having you help. Go sit down and put your feet up. I'll grab the car. It should take a half hour at most."

"You're fast."

"I've been doing this for a while."

He jogged to the car and pulled it into the garage then rolled the door shut behind him. While he worked, Betsy told him all about her day, starting with the funny e-mails she'd been getting, then onto the adventures with Chloe's neighbor. She finished with the bet on who could unearth the identity of their mystery reviewer.

"I'm still pretty sure it's Wes," said Betsy. "He said it wouldn't be the first person we thought of, but how could he know we'd think of him?"

"Are you sure it's a guy?"

"I think so. He said he was."

"He also said he was a time travelling zoologist from the future, so you might not be able to count on anything he-or she-is telling you."

"Ooh. You're right! What if it's a girl? Maybe it's Grace! She's secretly hilarious. You're good at this, by the way. Do you want to team up to figure it out?"

"Is that allowed?"

"No one said it wasn't. Besides, Chloe was just visiting the bookmobile to see if Wes would tip his hand, and she said she won't reveal her discoveries to 'the competition'."

"As long as it doesn't get me on Chloe's bad side, I'm in."

"It might, but only temporarily. You know how serious she is about her bets."

"She's intense about everything."

"Tell me about it. It works for her when she's focused on something productive. Now that she's with Arthur and she's putting the neighbor thing to rest, it should be smooth sailing. You wouldn't believe how her business has grown. She's totally rocking it."

Chloe would be a good person to talk to about running a business once the news about Karl taking over the shop had gotten out. Frank was sure to teach him a thing or two, but his lessons would necessarily be limited by his distaste for human interaction. "That's great," Karl said. "I'm so happy for her, and for you too. It seems like the perfect job for you."

"It is, and I'm thrilled for Chloe. She lights up every time she talks about her tools. I never saw her gush like this about her nine to five when she was working at that factory. It's been a lot of hard work, but I guess you have to fight for what you want sometimes."

And sometimes you have to let it go. Karl glanced back at Betsy, at the soft line of her jaw and the curve of her perfect lips. She smiled back at him, her dimples deepening. What was the worst thing that could happen if he walked over there right this minute, kneeled down in front of her, and kissed her? He could tell her how he felt, how he'd been feeling for years. How could he ever do enough to show her how much she meant to him, how much he wanted to mean to her?

He sighed. He was being selfish. She was with the father of her baby and had a fun new job with her sister. Her life was coming together.

If only Karl wasn't so certain that George was a loser who had likely-no, not likely, certainly-cheated on her with at least one other woman, probably two. If George thought Karl hadn't noticed when he'd left the bar early Friday night to go home with that tall brunette, he was mistaken. And hadn't Arthur said George was late because he was on the phone with some model?

Why did guys like that always get the girl? And not just any girl: Karl's best friend.

"I'm all finished here," he said.

"That was fast. You weren't kidding. I'm embarrassed it took me so long to bring it in."

Karl sat down next to her and handed Betsy her keys. He put his hand on her arm and kept it there. "Don't be afraid to ask for help. I'm always here for you. You know that, right?"

"I do. Thank you. You're the best. Now go home and eat some dinner."

"I've got to clean up here a little bit, but I'll do that." Once again he watched as Betsy drove away. When she hit the brakes and they didn't squeak, she gave Karl a thumb's up. He shot her one back, wrapped up the shop for the night, and started his walk home.

When he got back, Karl plopped down across the couch and pulled out his phone. Did he have any new e-mails? He checked his Gadgetgal account first. He'd gotten a message from Betsy.

Now that I'm sure you're someone we know (who else would anticipate our sister competition?), I have a question for you. I'm sure you and Dirk are very happy together, but do you ever wish you could've been with someone that you didn't want to replace with a shovel in the first place? Asking for a friend.

Best wishes, Betsy

Heart hammering in his chest, Karl tapped out a response.

Don't tell Dirk I said this, but you're a beautiful

person. You deserve someone who makes you happy, someone you don't want to replace with a shovel. Just because it's too late for me to have a sentient partner doesn't mean you should give up. You never know. Maybe the person you're looking for is right around the corner or a half mile down the road. On the other hand, you must be surrounded by shovels. You could take your pick of the finest.

A little bit of the pressure in Karl's chest relaxed. Apparently, Betsy was more clear-eyed about George than he'd thought.

Chapter Ten

In Which the Demeter Paranormal Society is Established

Just as Wes was starting to pack up for the day and head on out, Chloe raced in, followed by Lindsay and Sarah.

"I need your help," said Chloe as she strolled along the stacks of books.

Wes suppressed a sigh. He steeled himself, standing up tall and squaring his shoulders. "What can I help you with?"

Chloe grabbed a book off the shelf without looking at it. "I'm going to cut to the chase. Are you sending those funny e-mails?"

E-mails? "Nope. It's not me."

She wrinkled her forehead. "If it's not you, then who is it?"

"I couldn't tell you."

"Huh. Well, there goes my only lead. You'd tell me if it was you, right?"

"Sure. I really don't know anything about it. What kinds of e-mails are you getting? Do you mean funny like 'haha' or funny like 'strange'?"

"I mean 'haha' funny. Someone's sending fake reviews of my products every day, and Betsy and I have a bet on who'll be the first one to figure out who's behind them."

"Good luck. I'll let you know if I hear anything."

"Thanks."

Well, that was easy enough for Wes.

"And another thing..." Chloe continued. *Oh no.* It couldn't be that easy. When was Wes going to learn? "I have this neighbor. He never leaves the house. Groceries: dropped off. Car: maybe in the garage. I've never seen it. Garbage: cleaner takes it out and hauls it to the curb and back."

"Are you sure there's someone living there? Maybe it's a second home."

"No. It's not. The lights go on at night. Someone's in there."

"The lights could be on a timer."

Chloe looked at him like he was being a total killjoy, but wasn't that the most likely explanation? "The curtains twitch sometimes. They *twitch*, Wes."

"Did you try going over there and introducing yourself?"

"I did that today."

"And..."

"He answered on an intercom, because he thought I was a delivery person. He didn't open the door. I promised myself, Betsy too, that I'd let it go. I'm not going to bother him anymore. I'm only asking you because I thought he may have visited the library at some point. Maybe he would've gotten a library card. He moved here in February. His name's Noah

Clark."

Wes couldn't remember anyone by that name coming in as of late. There were a few newcomers who'd stopped in this year, but no Noahs as far as he could recall. "Sorry Chloe, no such luck." This was a rather inauspicious start to his grand plans to be helpful.

Lindsay, who'd been stocking up on romances with Sarah, chimed in. "Sorry, I couldn't help but hear you since we're all in the same bus and everything, and I've been having these really weird occurrences at the inn too."

"Like what?" Chloe asked, spinning around to face her.

"We have this nice older couple staying with us right now, and they're just as mystified as Grace and me."

"Tell us all about it." Chloe sat down on the stool, crossing her legs and resting her chin on her fist. She was prepared for a good story. "This is so weird. Maybe there's something going on around here: first my neighbor, then weird happenings at the inn. This can't be a coincidence." Sarah stopped leafing through her paperback to listen in as well.

"It started a few nights ago," Lindsay said. "I woke up one morning and every apple that had been in my fridge was on the table, with a single bite taken out of each one."

Chloe gasped. "Who did it?"

"I don't know. It was really awkward, but I had to ask my guests. I didn't think they would've done it, but the only other people there are Grace and me, and obviously it wasn't either of us. Our lodgers denied knowing anything, of course. They looked just as dumbfounded as we felt. It was embarrassing. What must they think about an inn where they're asked if they did something like that?"

"Yeah. You guys are pretty weird," joked Chloe. "Keep telling though." Wes was curious about what would happen next, too. This was nothing like any of the stories that usually made their way in here.

Lindsay continued. "I was dumbfounded, but what could I do? I went on with my day and assumed that would be the last of it."

"But it wasn't," Chloe predicted.

Lindsay laughed at her rapt expression. "No. It wasn't. The following day-this was yesterday-I woke up to ice cream on the table, completely melted with three spoons in it. Three!"

"Whoa," said Chloe. "The apples wouldn't have been such a big deal, but ice cream? I'd be mad. What kind was it?"

"Chocolate chip cookie dough."

Sarah gasped and Chloe shook her head. "What a waste."

"I know! And that wasn't the worst of it."

"Oh dear. I don't know if I can stand the suspense." Sarah stuck exclusively to romance novels with guaranteed happily ever afters.

"It was nothing awful," said Lindsay. "Just odd. Here it is: I made cinnamon rolls last night, the kind you put in the fridge overnight and then bake the next day."

"Please don't tell me..." said Chloe.

"Sorry, but I'm going to have to. They were out on the counter this morning. A bite was taken out of each one."

"Out of raw rolls? That's disgusting."

"Yes. Someone had pulled them out of the pan and left them on the table in a heap. It was a mess. Thankfully, I was able to clear it out before my guests came down for breakfast, otherwise it would've been really hard to explain why there was raw dough and butter smeared all over the table."

"How mysterious," said Sarah. "You ladies are always having adventures. And here I am: so tame with my paperback romances and good old Roy."

"I'd be happy not to have this kind of adventure," said Lindsay. Chloe chimed in to agree.

Being married to the outspoken and bombastic character that was Roy seemed like it would be an adventure in and of itself for Sarah, but Wes didn't say so. Instead, he seized the opportunity that had presented itself. "I can't solve any of your mysteries, but I *am* a librarian, so I can do what librarians do and offer you a book."

He knew exactly which one he'd recommend. It was perfect: a funny super kick-butt heroine, scary, but not terrifying. He scanned the stacks until he found the one he was looking for: spiky red lettering on a black spine. It was fortunate that he had three copies of the first book in the series. They usually flew out the door the moment they were returned, which was why he'd stocked up.

He presented a copy to each of the women in turn.

"I don't know," said Sarah, slipping on her reading glasses and peering at the back of the book with narrowed eyes. "This isn't the kind of thing I usually read."

"Me either," said Lindsay. "*A huntress on the trail of an ancient menace with diabolic cravings. Hauntingly tragic.* How is this supposed to make me less freaked out?"

Wes sat down on one of the stools. He pushed his glasses up on his nose, feeling confident in his authoritative librarian-ness. "I think the appeal to Sarah should be clear. It's a fantastic adventure. There's this police officer whose lover is killed under suspicious circumstances, and his body disappears before the funeral...I don't want to give too much away, but needless to say she becomes a vampire hunter." He gestured to the muscular stake wielding woman on the cover. "She's an incredible heroine, and the story's surprisingly emotionally complex. It's a paranormal romance."

Sarah looked unconvinced.

"Where do I come in?" Lindsay still wanted to know. "This sounds like, if anything, it'll scare me more."

Chloe was sold; she'd already started reading.

"You and Chloe are nervous about something in real life," said Wes, "and one of the best ways I've found to combat that is to read about something scary in a book. When you're reading in bed or on the couch, all wrapped up in blankets, you experience the fear in a safe space. You have control over it. It might help you put things in perspective. The heroine is also pretty tough, if you require a dose of courage."

"I'm totally sold," said Chloe. "Come on, you guys," she appealed to her two companions. "We can all read it together. I can't believe we hadn't thought of this before: a Demeter Society book club."

"Bea will never read this," said Lindsay. "She won't even watch A Christmas Carol because of the ghosts."

"Well, it doesn't have to be all of us. It can be us three. Please? It'll be so much fun."

Conceding, Sarah slid it on top of her stack of books.

"Yes! Lindsay, are you in?" Chloe asked.

"I suppose, but only because you two are reading it with me. If I'm terrified in the middle of the night, I'm calling you," Lindsay informed Chloe.

"Go for it. I'll be over in a heartbeat. It's not a bad idea to agree to leave our phones on at night. If it turns out you have a refrigerator vampire or I have an undead neighbor, we should be able to call each other."

"Don't call me," said Sarah. "If there are vampires invading the village, I'd rather not know. If my memory serves me right, they usually go for younger women anyway, so I should be safe."

"It's a deal," said Chloe. "This marks the first meeting of the Demeter Paranormal Romance Society." She examined the books next to the empty space on the shelf. "How many of these are there?"

"Fifteen," said Wes, "but they're not all in right now. It's a really popular series. The author's rumored to be working on the last one as we speak, but it's been two years since he released a book."

"That's alright; it'll take us a while to get through these." Chloe grabbed the next three books in the series and checked out. "See you fellow book clubbies," she said as she skipped out the door.

Lindsay and Sarah watched her go then checked out their own stacks of books. Both of them had chosen a pile of lighter fare as an antidote to Wes's suggestion. As a rule, he tried not to pay too much attention to what people read, but Wes couldn't miss the scores of Amish women and nineteenth century mail order brides on the covers of their other picks.

Having checked out and said goodbye to his two remaining customers, Wes closed up shop and headed for home. He waited for the pulse of panic to rise in his temples, but it never came. He'd really gone for it when it came to making book recommendations, so much so that a book club had sprung up. Had his pick been a good one? Chloe sure seemed to think so.

Maybe Wes was cut out for this responsibility stuff after all.

Chapter Eleven

In Which Betsy and Chloe Go on a Stake Out

In the middle of the night, Betsy was shaken awake. Someone was shining a cell phone light directly into her eyes. Screaming, she pushed herself up to sitting, trying to push the intruder away.

"Calm down. It's me." Chloe stood by the side of the bed.

Betsy struggled to bring her shuddering breath back to normal and pushed her hair out of her eyes. She shielded her face from the blinding light. "What are you doing here? Is something wrong?"

Chloe lowered the laser-like beam. "It's Lindsay. She called about ten minutes ago. I rushed over here right away."

"Oh my gosh. What happened? Is she okay?"

"They're okay at the moment, but there's someone banging around downstairs at the inn. The sound woke Lindsay up, and she called me to ask what she should do."

Betsy yawned. This had just gotten a lot less interesting. She wanted to go back to sleep. "It's obviously one of her guests. Doesn't that happen a lot? She tells people her kitchen's always open, and Grace said that a lot of their guests get up in the middle of the night to have a snack. Who knew?" Pulling her comforter over her head, Betsy waited for the sound of Chloe's retreating footsteps.

It never came.

Instead, Chloe yanked her blankets off then started pulling clothes out of the closet. She tossed a pair of black leggings and a tunic onto the bed. "Get dressed. We're going over there."

"Why?" Betsy groaned. "If she's really concerned, she should call the police. What could we possibly...Please tell me you don't have a pointy stick in your hand."

Chloe had called Betsy right before bed that night to tell her all about her new vampire book. Betsy had felt a glimmer of concern about the potential consequences of stoking Chloe's already fertile imagination, but to have it take effect so quickly...

Chloe flung both hands behind her back and slunk out the door. "Meet me downstairs."

"No, Chloe."

"Why? Don't you want to save the day?"

"Not particularly. I'm tired. I'm also annoyed that you broke into my house and terrified me. Couldn't you have called?"

"I did call, but you didn't answer."

"Because I was asleep! Besides, there's no reason to think someone's broken in, and if someone has, a pregnant woman and her sister, who is dressed in... are you wearing leather pants? Okay." Betsy slid out of bed and threw on her clothes. "I'm coming along just so you don't accidentally stab some innocent tourist."

Chloe punched the air. "Yes! Let's do this."

"See, saying that kind of thing in that tone of voice is exactly what you shouldn't do when you've just convinced me to drive over to our friends' house at one in the morning to investigate a noise."

"Okay. How about, this will be a boring visit to make sure our friends are safe and secure in their bed and breakfast."

"That's better."

"Look at us. Smoking hot vampire hunters." Chloe struck a pose, holding the stake above her head as if ready to strike, then strutted out of the room.

Betsy sighed and followed close behind.

"Can you drive?" Chloe asked. "I need to read you something."

"Sure." Betsy hopped into the driver's seat of Old Blue. Traveling over the winding back roads that led to Cherry Bounce Inn, Chloe filled Betsy in on the mysterious kitchen activity that had started a few nights ago. It was strange, there was no doubt about that, but there was probably some innocent explanation for the half-eaten food. Betsy couldn't imagine what that explanation could be, but that didn't mean there wasn't one.

"You said you wanted to read me something?" Betsy asked, not sure if she really wanted to hear it.

Chloe pulled a red and black paperback out of the glove box and flipped through the book until she found what she was looking for. "I know I said I was going to let this go, but listen to this: *Orpheus Adair lived alone, miles from the prying eyes of watchful neighbors. He'd tried to live in the city, unable to resist the temptation of warm slumbering bodies that lie unconscious in the rich velvety night, smooth unresisting necks awaiting his wicked red lips."*

"I don't remember you vowing to stop reading that book." It wouldn't be a terrible idea though, if their current circumstances were any indication.

"That's not all. Listen: *He hadn't counted on the inquisitiveness of human minds. Why, when his home appeared to be uninhabited, did flickering lights creep from beneath the curtains at night? Why had a fog of foreboding descended amongst the denizens of the borough at precisely the same moment that the For Sale sign had disappeared from his decrepit brownstone?"*

"So this is the famous vampire book?" Betsy asked, swiping it from Chloe's hand.

Chloe snatched it back. "Keep your eyes on the road. But yes, Wes said that reading something scary would take my mind off the creepy things going on in real life."

Betsy thought he couldn't have picked a more unfortunate title. "Maybe we should return this one and find something that hits a little less close to home."

"No way. This book is incredible. The woman on the cover? Her name is Nina Striker."

"Really?"

"Yes, really. She leaps from rooftops, stalks dark alleys and abandoned graveyards…"

"So the usual everyday stuff?"

"Sort of, but it's also really emotional. Her one true love has been turned into a vampire, and there's some part of him that still loves her, but they're pitted against each other in this epic battle for innocent souls. They're star-crossed lovers."

"And this was supposed to make you *less* concerned about the neighbor?"

"I don't think Wes realized how closely the descriptions were going to match my reality."

"But you're still not going to bother the neighbor again, right? Because vampires aren't really part of your reality."

"I'm not. I promise, but I'm more convinced that ever that there's something odd going on in this village."

"Chloe..." Betsy said warningly.

Chloe held up her hands in defense of her sanity. "I'm not delusional, but it's kind of fun to imagine I'm Nina, slipping into that little Cape Cod during the day while Noah's asleep in his coffin, hordes of rats with beady red eyes pouring out of the bathroom."

"But you're not going to do that, because you're not Nina, and your neighbor's not a vampire." Was it insulting to Chloe that Betsy wanted this much clarity on whether she knew she wasn't a fictional vampire hunter?

"Of course I'm not her. I'm blonde. Now where did I stash that stake? Oh, here it is." She reached down between her feet and set it across her lap.

When they pulled up to the inn, a red brick Belgian farmhouse that had been in Lindsay and Grace's family for over a century, all was quiet. They were surrounded by dark fields. Thick hardwood forests crouched in the far distance. The lights in the house were out. There was no sign of movement anywhere. If Betsy didn't know better, she'd assume that everyone inside was asleep, but there were at least two people awake that they knew of: Lindsay and whoever was making those noises downstairs.

Lindsay was likely still in bed, staring into the darkness while she waited for them to arrive. If she really was that scared, Betsy was glad to stop by, but she still thought it might've been smarter to have called someone less...Chloe had already hopped out of the truck and was slinking along the wall.

Stepping down to the driveway, Betsy closed the door softly behind her. She decided against the slinking route and walked straight to the back steps, which led directly to the kitchen. Reaching the back porch, she peeked in the window next to the door then leaped back, joining Chloe on the side of the house.

"There's someone in there."

Chloe's eyes widened. "In the dark?"

"He's standing by the table, not moving. It's creepy."

"Could you tell who it was?"

"No, but I'm certain it's a man. We should call the police."

"Where's the fun in that?"

"Chloe."

"You're probably right, but let me take a look

first."

Once again, Chloe edged her way along the wall until she reached the stairs. She leaped them two by two and crouched beneath the window. Why didn't she hurry up? What had seemed like a lark before had become more ominous now that Betsy had seen the tall dark figure looming over the table.

Chloe popped up, cupped her hands against the glass, and peered inside. She jumped back down the steps and rejoined Betsy on the side of the house. "He's gone," she said. "I don't see anyone in there. Are you sure you saw someone?"

"I'm positive. Let's call the police now, okay? If it was one of her lodgers, they wouldn't have been standing there in the dark like that."

"What if it's too late by the time they get here? If he's disappeared, he's either gone into the living room or up the stairs to the bedrooms."

She had a point. They couldn't just sit out here while someone crept around the inn. "This is scary," said Betsy. "We should've told Lindsay to call the police from the start."

"But we didn't. We have to go in there."

Betsy got on her phone and called Officer Anselme, Grace's boyfriend. He answered right away, and Betsy explained what was going on. "I'm a couple miles away. I'll be over in five minutes," he said. "Tell Chloe to sit tight."

"I'll try."

But it was too late. When Betsy turned around, Chloe was gone. The door to the kitchen swung closed with a click.

Betsy stared down the dark house, frozen to the spot. What should she do? Go inside? Her sister was alone in there, but it was ridiculous that she'd gone inside without discussing it first. Chloe had to have known Betsy would try to talk her out of it, and with good reason.

It might not be safe in there, and being alone made it even less so.

Betsy had to go into the house. It might be foolish, and she couldn't believe this was where her early night had ended up taking her, but she wouldn't be able to live with herself if something happened to Chloe while she had been standing outside deliberating.

Betsy raced up the stairs and flung open the door. Her eyes had already adjusted to the darkness. Was there anyone in the kitchen? Not that she could tell.

Which way had Chloe gone? The stairs were the most logical choice. If she and Chloe reached Lindsay and Grace without coming across the intruder, they could all hang tight until Officer Anselme arrived. Betsy slipped off her shoes and tiptoed across the polished wood floor.

"Chloe?" she whispered into the darkness.

No answer.

She crept up the stairs, listening. Hushed voices were coming from Lindsay's bedroom. Betsy tried the door. It was locked. She tapped lightly, and the voices stopped. Halting footsteps approached the door.

"Who is it?" whispered Grace.

"It's me, Betsy," she whispered back, scanning the eerily dark hallway. "Let me in."

Grace flung open the door and pulled Betsy inside, locking it behind her. "Sorry. We didn't know you were coming into the house."

Lindsay and Chloe sat at the edge of the bed with flashlights in their hands. Grace and Betsy joined them.

"Did you call Dave?" Chloe asked.

Betsy nodded. "He'll be here any minute."

"Did you see anyone out there?"

"No. I wouldn't be sitting here calmly if I did. Why did you leave me out there?"

"Because I knew you'd tell me to wait, and I didn't want to."

Just as she'd thought. Oh well, at least Chloe was honest.

Grace went to the window. "Here he is! I'll call him and tell him we're in Lindsay's room."

Moments later, there was another knock at the bedroom door, louder this time. "It's me."

Grace ran to the door and opened it, and Betsy swore she had never been so happy to see the face of Dave Anselme in her life. He slipped inside, closing the door behind him.

"You four stay here. I'm going to look around. I didn't see anyone down there, but I assume you didn't leave a pile of open yogurt containers on your table overnight."

Just then there was another knock at the door.

Betsy tensed.

"Hello?" It was a woman's voice. Dave opened the door again, startling an elderly blonde woman in a green and pink striped bathrobe. Upon seeing the crowd in the bedroom, she threw her hand to her heart. Her eyes seemed to double in size. "Oh my. What's going on?"

Lindsay stepped forward. "I'm so sorry about this. We heard noises downstairs, so we called Officer Anselme to make sure there was no one in the house."

Betsy had expected the woman to react with shock or concern, but she looked bashful instead. "Oh, this is awful. I'm sorry. I should've said something sooner, but my husband is so embarrassed about his sleepwalking."

Everyone else looked as flabbergasted as Betsy felt.

"He never does it at home, and we hadn't slept anywhere else in a while, so we were hoping it had stopped, but when we saw those apples on your counter…" Her chin trembled; she pulled up her robe to meet it. "I wanted to tell you so you wouldn't be frightened, but Richard insisted it hadn't been him. I knew it was, of course, but he's so touchy about it."

"Is he back in bed?" Dave asked.

"He's sound asleep."

"That's fine. Don't wake him up." Dave turned to Lindsay. "Do you want to go downstairs and check out the kitchen?"

With Dave leading the way, everyone (except for the slumbering Richard) clumped into the kitchen, where at least twenty individual yogurt containers were open, with a scoop out of each. A whole drawer full of spoons was littered across the table; a few had even made it to the floor.

"Wow," said Grace. "He really went to town with those yogurts."

"Oh. I am so sorry," the woman said again. She tugged the belt on her robe tighter around her waist. "We'll pay for the food, and I can help you clean up." She gathered up some of the spoons, tossing them into the sink.

"Please don't worry about it," said Lindsay. "This is your last night here, and it's been lovely having you. I'd be most grateful if you headed back up to bed and got a good night's sleep. We'll pretend this never happened."

"But we've caused you so much trouble, and this nice officer, and a pregnant woman, and this other woman in leather pants had to come all the way out here, all because of us."

"Really. It's fine," said Lindsay, taking over at the sink. "I could tell you stories about other guests that make sleepwalking sound like you're doing me a favor. Trust me."

The woman looked at Lindsay dubiously, but shuffled back up the stairs anyway.

Grace put both hands on Dave's uniformed chest and stood on her tiptoes to kiss him. "I don't mind getting to see you tonight, but sorry we called you out here for something silly."

"Don't worry about it. I'd rather come over for

a false alarm than not have you call me at all. You shouldn't have gone into the house, by the way," he said to Chloe. "I think you know that."

Chloe, who must've stashed her stake somewhere in Lindsay's bedroom said, "I know, but what if it *had* been an intruder?"

Dave sighed. "I appreciate your protective instinct, but it would've been better if you'd have called me right away."

"I'll keep that in mind," Chloe said, but her eyes darted in a way that revealed to those who knew her well that she was still in Nina Striker mode.

Betsy sat down at the table, too tired to stand.

"You look exhausted," said Grace. "Go on home. We've got this. Thanks so much for coming out here, you two."

"Any time," said Chloe.

"Or you can call me so I can do my job," said Dave. "You know. The one I'm trained to do."

"Doesn't it help to have backup though?" Chloe asked. "Someone who can operate outside the law?"

"No," said Dave.

Chloe looked crestfallen. "Fine then, but I hope your training included how to deal with things outside of the natural world."

"It did. I'm not allowed to talk about it." His radio crackled to life. He headed for the door. "I've got to run, but I'm glad everyone's alright. See you tomorrow night?" he asked Grace.

"Absolutely. I can't wait." He kissed her one last time before he left.

"Do you want any help cleaning up?" Chloe asked.

"You two go on home. This won't take long at all. It's a little yogurt and a few spoons." Grace grabbed a washcloth and wiped clods of yellow, pink, and blue from the tabletop.

Chloe probably would've objected, but Betsy stood up and put on her shoes. "Goodnight guys," she said. "It's been interesting." She concealed a yawn behind the back of her arm.

Lindsay and Grace saw them out the door, and Chloe hopped behind the wheel for the drive home.

"Sorry about the false alarm," said Chloe, pulling up to Betsy's house. Betsy couldn't believe how quickly they'd gotten there. She must've nodded off.

"It's okay. Sorry about being late for work tomorrow."

"I deserve that. See you at ten?"

"Deal."

Betsy unlocked the door, climbed the stairs, peeled off her leggings, and fell asleep in an instant.

***

At 10:15 the following morning, Betsy got the e-mail from Gadgetgal. When she'd called last night, before their midnight adventure, Chloe had wasted no time in telling her that their mystery person wasn't Wes and grilling Betsy on whether she'd gotten any leads. Betsy had said, truthfully, that she had absolutely no idea who'd been sending those e-mails.

Until now.

Betsy typed out a reply.

I know someone who's worth more than all the shovels put together, and he does live right down the street. By the time I came around to realizing that we belonged together, it was too late. His life is complicated, and he needs someone whose love will make it simpler. Maybe that could've been me, once upon a time, but it isn't anymore. I made the wrong choice, a lot of wrong choices. I've messed everything up. I'm so sorry.

Throat burning, she deleted the message before she could hit send. Why hadn't she figured it out sooner? Karl was right in front of her all this time.

He'd had to grow up way too soon, while she carried on with her nonsense well past its expiration date. One good thing had come out of her bad choices, though, and there was still plenty of time to keep up her positive forward progress.

Betsy cradled her stomach and felt her baby press against her ribs. What would her little girl be like? She'd been active around the clock lately, and Betsy loved to lie in bed and watch her stomach shift and wiggle. Her little girl was already more loved than she could ever know.

Turning her attention back to the computer, Betsy was about to type out a new response to Gadgetgal when her phone rang.

It was Karl.

She hadn't accidentally sent that e-mail, had she?

Grabbing her phone off the table, she answered it, trying to sound casual. "Hey. What's up?"

"Betsy?" It came out in a gasp. It sounded like he'd been crying.

"What's wrong?"

"It's Nick. He was hit by a car when he was biking down Main Street."

Betsy gasped. *No. Please no. Please not Nick.* "Is he okay?"

"He was able to call me," said Karl. "But I'm not sure. By the time I got to him, the ambulance had already taken him to the hospital in Sturgeon Bay. I'm on my way."

Betsy was already getting up to leave. "I'll be there as soon as I can."

Chapter Twelve

In Which Karl Gets a String of Bad News

When Karl walked into the shop earlier that morning, Frank didn't say a word as he passed by, and he didn't respond when Karl offered his usual brief greeting. That was odd.

Not stopping to find out if it was him or something else that was the source of Frank's sour mood, Karl headed into the shop. Had a problem come up with selling the garage? Along with the after effects of his meeting with Betsy, Karl had thought of very little else other than the prospect of being the owner of the shop.

He admired Frank and the way he ran things, but Karl had some ideas of his own to modernize a bit that he thought Frank would approve of. He'd never been brave enough to make any suggestions while he was still an underling; Frank wasn't the kind of boss who would welcome that kind of input, but once Karl was in charge, he could make some changes that would make an already great business even better.

As he popped the hood of his first truck of the day, however, Karl couldn't shake the feeling that something was wrong. Frank was a man of few words, but he always greeted Karl in some way or another as he walked through the door, even if it was nothing but a grunt of acknowledgement.

An hour went by with no sign of Frank, no indication of what could be wrong. Karl could hear him dealing with customers in the office. He sounded short-tempered. That was odd. Frank was never rude to customers. Just when Karl had decided he couldn't take it any more and was going to march into that office and ask Frank what was going on, Frank came marching the other way.

Karl stiffened. The air felt heavy around him. Frank stopped ten feet from the truck Karl was working on. He took a wide stance and put his hands on his hips, the way he did when he was dealing with a particularly disgruntled customer. "Gotta ask you about something."

Karl stopped working and turned to face him. "Sure," he said, trying to sound relaxed, like the blood hadn't just rushed to his head, making his face tingle and his ears buzz.

"When did you shut down the shop last night?"

"Shortly after you left. I had one more job to finish up, like I said."

"Huh. Well, Ed called me last night. He saw lights on in the shop until almost 8. Wanted to make sure somebody hadn't broken in. I came over to check it out, but nothing was missing."

Karl was caught. Betsy didn't have to be though. He'd promised her he wouldn't say anything to her dad. Frank loved his three girls, but he wasn't easy on them, especially Betsy.

"I'm sorry. It was me in the shop. I didn't leave until almost 8."

"So, you lied to me just now?"

"There was someone who was in need, and I agreed to help them."

"How many times have you done this? Are you doing extra work on the side at my garage?"

"No. I've never done anything like this before."

Frank didn't look angry. He didn't look anything. His face was completely neutral as he said, "I'm going to need to talk to this person to see if your story checks out. I've never known you to be dishonest before, but once someone lies to me, that's it."

"I'm sorry. I can't tell you who it was. They didn't want anyone to know, and I don't want to betray their trust."

"But you're comfortable with betraying mine?" Frank's voice rose, his jaw stiffened.

"No. I'm not, but I promised I wouldn't say anything."

"What about your agreement to work for me during business hours? How do I know you haven't been pulling this stuff for months, lining your pockets at my expense?"

Karl couldn't believe that was even in question. He'd been working there for over a year, and this was what Frank thought of him? "I don't know what to say. I'd never do that."

"Then tell me whose car you were working on. If it's true that they needed help, they'll tell me. You'll have nothing to worry about."

There was still a chance for Karl to salvage his hopes of getting the shop, of making life easier for him, his parents, and Nick. It would change everything for them, but at what cost? He'd given his word.

He stayed silent.

Frank stared him down, his eyes narrowed. He didn't say another word as he strode back into the office. That was it. Karl had been given the privilege of thinking things were looking up for less than twenty-four hours, and he'd been proven wrong in the worst possible way. This was what came from reaching for something more. He should've known it was too good to be true. He wouldn't be at all surprised if he lost his job as well. At this point, it would be a miracle if he didn't.

A bland numbness encircled him as he got back to work. When he was almost finished with his second car of the day, Karl's phone rang on the desk. He ran over, slamming his shin on a metal drawer that he must've left open. He winced as he reached for his phone. No one ever called him during the day, unless it was a telemarketer or an emergency. It was Nick.

"Hey man, what's up?"

"Karl?" Nick groaned.

Karl's stomach dropped like he'd just missed the last step. "What's wrong? What happened?" There was no answer. "Nick? Answer me."

When Nick finally spoke again, his voice sounded wavery and far away. "I was on my bike. I think my leg's broken."

"Where are you?"

"Almost to Martel's...it came out of nowhere."

The shriek of an ambulance pierced the silent shop, roaring by when it passed then receding into the distance. It was heading for Martel's Grocery and Nick.

"I'll be right there." Karl hung up, grabbed his keys, and ran out the open garage door.

By the time Karl reached the spot where his brother had been struck, Nick had been taken away in the ambulance. Officer Anselme was there, talking into this two-way radio and stringing up caution tape around the scene of the accident. It wasn't difficult to miss. Blood streaked the curb and soaked into the road. Nick's old Schwinn was unmistakable, black with streaks of blue. Its back tire was so mangled it had been bent almost in half.

"What happened?" Karl yelled, pushing through the caution tape and confronting Dave.

Dave met Karl next to the bike. "Nick's going to be alright. They've taken him to the hospital in Sturgeon Bay."

"Who did this?" A red haze of fury was forming at the edges of his vision. Karl spotted a tall pimply teenager talking with another officer. His bony shoulders were hunched; he stared at the ground as he spoke, barely moving his lips. "Is that the guy who did this?"

"You need to calm down. Go meet Nick at the hospital."

"Calm down? My brother's just been hit by some idiot kid and you're telling *me* to calm down?"

"We're interviewing the driver right now. I can't say anything more than that. Please. He's going to want you there. We've got this under control." He lowered his voice and put his hand on Karl's shoulder. "Nick's going to be alright. He was talking and joking around with the paramedics. He got a nasty gash on his leg, but I'm positive you'll feel better when you see him."

Karl jerked away from Dave and sprinted back to his truck. He couldn't get there as fast as the ambulance, but they must've just left. He thought about calling his parents. His mom was at work right now, his dad probably sitting by the window in the living room. He pictured their already careworn faces, stricken by grief and fear when they heard the news.

He'd go to the hospital first and see how Nick was doing. Once Karl saw him and knew what kind of state he was in, he'd call his parents. He couldn't wait too long, or someone in town was bound to get in touch with them, but it wouldn't take him more than twenty minutes to reach the hospital if he hurried.

Who else could he call? He felt panicky, like he needed to talk to someone.

Betsy.

Betsy would want to know what happened. She'd drop everything and be there almost as quickly as he would. In fact, she'd probably be furious if he didn't call her.

Just when he thought she wasn't going to answer, Betsy picked up. Karl told her what had happened and, as he'd expected, she said she'd be right behind him.

Even though Karl drove as fast as he could, the trip felt like it took an hour. Karl screeched into the parking lot, flew into the emergency room entrance, and slid up to the reception desk.

He didn't wait for the bespectacled woman behind the desk to look up. "A kid named Nick Barber was brought in. I'd like to see him."

"Of course. Are you family?"

"I'm his brother."

"One minute. I'll check if I can take you back."

Karl waited. A television on the wall played a daytime talk show. It was muted; subtitles scrolled across the bottom of the screen. The room was stuffy, empty, and smelled of disinfectant. Karl didn't want to be here. He didn't want Nick to be here.

The receptionist returned. "Follow me," she said. "He said to tell you 'it looks worse than it is'."

When Karl reached his brother, he sincerely hoped that was true. Nick was lying nearly flat on a hospital bed with a blood-soaked bandage around his leg. Both his arms were scratched, rubbed raw in some places. His bottom lip was split and his right eye was almost completely swollen shut. "You made it for the party," said Nick. He tried to sit up, winced, and leaned back again.

"Sorry I didn't get more dressed up for the occasion," said Karl.

"It's a come-as-you-are affair."

Karl grabbed a chair and pulled it up next to his brother's head. He was so happy to hear Nick joking around that he wanted to cry with relief. "What happened? Given the state of your bike, you actually look pretty good."

"Hey, thanks," said Nick, framing his face with his hands and giving his brother a cheesy grin. He grimaced. "It even hurts to smile. Anyway, I was on my way to work, biking along with traffic, when a car drove up and hit me from behind. I was thrown clear off my bike then scraped along the road a bit until the curb and my head stopped my momentum. Good thing I was wearing a helmet. I think I might've passed out for a minute, but it could've been a lot worse. The next thing I remember the paramedics were there."

"Is anything broken?"

"They don't think so. My leg hurts like crazy. I'll need stitches. Can you believe it? My first stitches."

"I'll take photos so you have a memento."

"Thanks, but I think I'll pass. Do Mom and Dad know?"

"I haven't called them yet. I wanted to see how you were doing first."

"Good thinking."

"I'll call them now. Do you want to be the one to talk to them?"

"I think I'd better. Let's try Dad. He's more likely to be able to answer."

Karl dialed his dad, handing the phone to Nick. "Dad?" said Nick. He told him all about what had happened. His dad promised to get in touch with his mom. They'd be up as soon as they could.

A nurse walked in. "Your wife is here," she said to Karl. "Should I tell her to come back, or do you want to meet her at reception?"

Karl was about to say there'd been a mistake when Nick chimed in. "Tell her she can come back. It'll make me feel a lot better to see Karl's wife."

"Sounds good. I'll let her know. I told her she could come back, but she said you two might want some time alone together first."

Karl understood now. Only family was allowed back here.

"Isn't that interesting?" asked Nick. "She could've said she was my sister, but she chose to be your wife instead."

Karl tried to hold back his look of pure satisfaction, but the effort was useless.

"Before she gets back here, I need to say something." Nick turned his head on the pillow to face Karl.

"Not if it's about Betsy and me," said Karl. "We've been through this."

"Humor me. I was just hit by a car."

What could Karl say to that? The kid had a point. "Alright. Go ahead."

"I was thinking about it on the way here, for obvious reasons. You're always telling me to go for what I want; to take chances and bet on myself."

"Yes?"

"Well, what about you?"

"What about me?" Karl suspected he knew

where Nick was going with this.

"You say you've tried to tell Betsy how you feel, but have you really? I mean, like, actually told her?" Karl started to reply, but Nick interrupted him. "Don't bother. I know you haven't. And do you want to know how I know? Because you two aren't together, and you should be. And do you know *why* I think you haven't tried? Because you're afraid of having something, someone, who would be that precious to you. She could be snatched away in an instant, any time at all. We both know that better than most. Look at what happened today." He gestured to his bloody face. "But what's the alternative? Never having anything important enough that you'd care if it was gone? That's just sad. If you expect me to go for what I want, I want to see you doing the same thing. Life's too short."

Karl had an objection ready, but he stopped as the truth of what Nick said hit him like a sock to the gut. Karl thought he was trying to protect Betsy, but was he protecting himself just as much, if not more?

"Hey guys, I hope I'm not intruding." Betsy peeked into the room.

"Come on in," said Nick. "It's my favorite sister-in-law. Congratulations, you two! I'm a little peeved you didn't invite me to the wedding, but I'll get over it."

A nurse, who had just come in and was writing something on the white board, squinted at the three of them out of the corner of her eye before striding out of the room.

"Very funny," Betsy replied. "I was put on the spot. How are you feeling?"

Nick assured her that he felt better than he looked as well, but Karl wasn't so sure. Nick had a tendency to put everyone else's comfort above his own. Karl also wasn't sure how he'd be able to look Betsy in the eye after that speech from Nick. Once again, Nick may have been right, but what did it matter now? It was too late. Karl had missed his chance.

Today had started out rough, but he was so happy to see Nick alive and relatively well that everything else that had happened-the confrontation at the shop, the awful scene on the side of the road-faded into the distance as Karl watched his brother joke around with Betsy. He looked terrible, but he would be back to normal in no time-he'd already found the strength to bug Karl about Betsy again, so that had to be a positive sign.

Karl laughed as Nick launched into one of his favorite grocery store tales. Without looking over at him, Betsy took Karl's hand in hers. They laced their fingers together. Nick held Karl's gaze for a moment then carried on with his story. Karl had heard it a million times, but he'd happily hear it a million more.

Chapter Thirteen

In Which Advice Has Unforeseen Consequences

Later that afternoon, Wes sat at the kitchen table in the farmhouse at Cedar Hollow Farm. It was so comfortable and warm; it felt natural that it would soon be his home. Faded floral wallpaper stuck neatly to expansive walls. On the table, creamy white peonies drooped in a glass vase whose watery blue tint could only be seen in just the right light. Lace curtains hung loosely above a wide ceramic sink, canisters of flour, sugar, and coffee sat on a thick oak shelf, and a fat pink teakettle perched on the metal grate of an old gas range.

Bea set the last pie on top of a stack that was already eight high. "Thanks for agreeing to deliver these. You're a lifesaver."

"I'm happy to do it, as long as you don't mind if they don't all make it to their destination. I went far too long without access to Belgian pies. They're hard for me to resist. What kind do you have here, anyway?"

"They're rice, prune, and cherry. I've written what kind they are and who they should go to on the top to make it easier for you."

"And it's Cherry Bounce Inn first, Emma's second."

"Right." Bea passed the stack to Wes as her mom came into the kitchen. Claudette wore a vintage polka dotted tea length skirt and draping sapphire top with comfortable sandals. Bea and her mom looked so much alike it was almost uncanny.

Wes said hello and offered Claudette a chair next to him. She took a seat while Bea poured her a cup of tea.

"Are you going to take a walk this afternoon, Claudette?" Wes asked. "Bea said you might head over to the pond."

"Oh, I don't know," she replied vaguely. "I suppose so." She took a sip of her hot chamomile tea.

"I have to help Dad out in the barn, but then we can walk on the path through the meadow," Bea said to her mom as she poured herself a cup of tea and sat down next to her.

"You can head out, Wes. Mom and I will visit for a bit."

Kissing them each on the cheek, Wes said goodbye, picked up the pile of pies, and headed out to the bookmobile. It was parked in front of the barn, next to the fence that kept in the goats.

Goatzart stuck her head out for a scratch and Wes obliged. It seemed silly, but he used to be a bit nervous about petting the goats. With their chomping teeth and their bulging eyes, they had a look of danger about them, but he was currently on a friendly first name basis with nearly every one of them.

Once he'd learned that they all have their own

personalities and funny quirks, just like people, he was sold. The chickens and cats were the same way.

Who knew?

Opening the passenger door, Wes piled some of the pies on the seat and the rest on the floor. He eased onto the county highway and drove down the road. It was a gorgeous drive to Cherry Bounce Inn, surrounded as it was by other farms with cherry and apple orchards of their own.

He passed a sweet little roadside chapel and some farm kids chasing each other across a grassy field. Bea had loved growing up on the farm, and Wes had been over at Cedar Hollow so often that he felt like he'd grown up there too, climbing in the trees, sneaking into the haymow, and wrangling the barn cats. It was a perfect place to raise a family.

When he arrived at the inn, Wes pulled up the driveway and parked near the barn.

He couldn't believe he'd be celebrating there, as a married man no less, in a matter of weeks. Since yesterday evening, when he'd given those books to Lindsay, Chloe, and Sarah, he'd been feeling more confident about all of the changes coming his way.

Wes grabbed three of the pies: one cherry, one prune, and one rice, and carried them up the back stairs. He tapped on the door with his elbow, not wanting to risk balancing the pies with one hand.

Lindsay opened the door and invited him inside. Setting the pies on her kitchen table, Wes asked, "How's it going?"

"So-so." Lindsay was in yoga pants and a t-shirt. There were dark bags under her eyes.

Was something wrong? "Did you start the vampire book?" he asked.

"Did I? I was up half the night thanks to that book."

Some of Wes's optimism drained away. "Was it really that scary? I don't remember it being too bad."

Lindsay yawned and rubbed her eyes. She filled Wes in on what had happened the night before, starting with the mysterious sounds in the kitchen, and ending with a panicked call to Officer Anselme and a sleepwalking lodger.

That wasn't what Wes had intended to happen, but it wasn't the book's fault, surely.

"Chloe showed up in leather pants wielding a stake," Lindsay added.

So maybe it was partly the book's fault.

But Lindsay would have been worried about mysterious thumps in the night anyway. Anyone would have. It was possible they never would've discovered the sleepwalker if they hadn't been brave enough to investigate. Chloe was taking it to a whole new level, though. He guessed he should've anticipated that. "I take it you want to return the book?" he asked.

"I think I'd better. Would you mind taking it back now? I'm afraid to even have it in the house tonight."

"I don't mind at all, and if my memory serves me right, you have plenty of sweet romances to get you back into a calmer state of mind."

"That's true. I couldn't sleep when I got back into bed after the clean-up, so I read one of my old favorites." Lindsay ran upstairs and came back with the mischief inducing book. "Thanks for trying. It wasn't the right answer for me, but Chloe will undoubtedly be back for the whole series."

"Is that a good thing?"

"Only time will tell...but probably not."

Wes left Lindsay's kitchen a bit less confident than he'd been going into it, but he still had another stop to make. He couldn't let this hiccough get him down. There would be some hits and some misses. The vampire book just happened to be a miss.

Ten minutes later, Wes arrived at Emma's Café with the other six pies. Bea delivered pies to Emma's nearly every day, and they sold out almost immediately after their arrival.

Wes was strolling around the side of the bus when an irate Roy shot out the door and headed straight for him.

"Jacquemart! I need to have a word with you."

Roy, who was nearly as wide as he was tall, walked right up to Wes and pushed him in the chest. It wasn't enough to knock him over, but it was startling nonetheless. Roy was at least thirty years older than Wes, but Wes was a realist when it came to who would win in any kind of a physical confrontation, and it wasn't the bespectacled librarian.

Before Wes could ask what he'd done to deserve the shove, Roy cleared it up for him. "Sarah was reading some kind of book about a hunter woman last night. She was all secretive about it, but I saw it on the nightstand after she went to sleep. It looks like smut to me. Is that the kind of thing you're handing out from the village's bookmobile these days?"

Wes gulped but didn't say anything, not wanting to make it worse. Roy was the village board president and could make things difficult if he had a mind to, which he often did.

"I wasn't overly concerned," Roy continued. "Thought it must be a passing fad or something those Demeter Society ladies roped her into, but this morning Sarah was out the door before she could make me a hot breakfast. I found a note on the counter. Do you want to know what it said?"

Not really, but it didn't seem like Wes was being given a choice. "It said, 'Gone to the Y. Lifting weights with friends. Don't wait for breakfast.' I went back upstairs to take a peek at that book again and, sure enough, there's a muscular woman on the cover, giving my wife ideas."

Roy stared at Wes, panting as if ready to fight, and Wes considered that now might be a good time to say something if he wanted to save his neck. "What happened was..."

"I'm not finished," Roy interrupted. "I still wanted my usual hot breakfast: eggs, with bacon, Canadian bacon, and sausage on the side, so I came over to Emma's. Keep in mind, at this point I'm so hungry I could eat a horse. I plop myself down in my usual booth and order my usual breakfast. What do you think Emma said?"

"Coming right up?" Wes ventured hopefully.

"No. That's not what she said at all. She said something more like, 'We're no longer serving cured meats because of the nit-, nitro- something or others.' She offered me 'smoky maple tofu bacon'. I don't even know what that is. Do you know what that is, Wes? Does anyone?"

"No?" Although Wes had some guesses, no felt like the safest answer.

"No. No one knows what that is, and they shouldn't. I asked her what she'd done with the real bacon, the kind that came from a pig, and do you know what she said?"

"That it was gone?"

"That's right. It was gone. And do you know what? That tofu bacon, it was disgusting. I didn't touch it. I went home and made a bowl of cereal. Those eggs only held me over for so long. Now I'm back for dinner and guess what?"

"No meat?"

"You've got it. Which brings me to why we're standing out here in the parking lot together, having this friendly chat."

Wes hoped that would be explained eventually. "I asked her why," said Roy. "Why did she change the menu all of a sudden, leaving the poor people of this fine community without their favorite meats? And do you know what she told me? She told me that you lent her a vegetarian cookbook. A cookbook full of recipes with no meat. I don't understand how such a thing is even possible."

Roy stared down Wes as if waiting for another answer, but Wes didn't know what to say. He'd tried going vegetarian for a while and had grown quite fond of chickpeas in the process, but once again, he knew that wasn't the correct answer.

"I don't know about you, Jacquemart," said Roy, shaking his head. "This is a dangerous game you're playing, monkeying with a man's breakfast and dinner foods."

Wes finally spoke up. "The vegetarian thing is probably just a phase Emma's going through because it's new to her. Give her a couple of weeks, and she'll be back to serving up piles of bacon fried in butter."

"A couple of *weeks*?" Roy clearly couldn't believe what he was hearing. "I'll give her two days, and then I'm taking action." He stomped away, leaving Wes frozen to the spot in front of the bookmobile, wondering what kind of action could reasonably be taken. Maybe Roy could use those table cloths from the bacon themed wedding as a banner and stage a protest in front of the café...

Wes snapped out of it and grabbed the remaining pies. There wasn't much he could do about Emma. He *had* introduced her to the cookbook, but he couldn't have known she would take it to heart so quickly. He'd only recommended it to her yesterday morning. And as for Sarah, Wes was actually happy to hear that she was going out and doing something for herself. Maybe Roy would be forced to learn how to make his own bacon and eggs for once.

Inside the café, Wes was greeted with the scent

of hot coffee and burnt garlic. The early dinner crowd created a murmur of friendly chatting and laughter mingled with the clink of forks and knives against serviceable white plates. Emma, who had been running from table to table with a tray balanced in each hand, swept past Wes then backtracked when she saw what he was holding.

"You're the pie delivery man today, eh Wes?"

"I sure am."

"Perfect timing. These folks are going to want dessert. You know where they go, right?"

"Of course." Wes headed back into the kitchen where an empty shelf that was especially reserved for the Belgian pies was positioned smack dab in the middle of the big commercial refrigerator.

Ernie, Emma's husband and the café's longtime cook, cleared his throat just as Wes was about to leave. Wes froze. He pivoted to face Ernie, who was at least as big as Roy but about a twentieth as belligerent, usually. Today, however, he appeared to be giving Roy a run for his money in the disgruntled department.

"Vegetarian, huh?" Ernie asked.

"Roy and I just discussed this. I'm sorry. I didn't realize that Emma would be become so passionate about vegetarian cuisine. People out there seem to be enjoying it."

"They'd better. Do you know how much work it is to chop veggies for 100 meals on your own? Fries? Easy. Burgers? Easy. West African peanut soup with kale? Not so easy. Want to stay and help?"

"I really would, but I have to run." *As far away as possible from the cook with the wickedly sharp knife.*

Wes took to his heels and bolted out the door before he could be accosted by any more angry villagers. Most of the diners in the café had looked pleased with their meals, but Wes felt a couple of angry looks being sent in his direction as he darted out the door. He passed the red benches, skirted around the baskets of petunias hanging from the eaves of the red metal roofed building, and had almost made it to the bus when someone else called out to him from the direction of the benches.

Who was mad at him now?

It was Patrick. Wes hadn't noticed him in his rush to escape to the safety of his library. Patrick, who looked and sounded like he should've been a fellow librarian, was one of Chloe's neighbors. He could often be found tossing cracked corn to the geese in the park off of Main Street or sitting on this very bench with Tom, laughing and listening to tall tales. Today, however he was completely alone.

Not having given Patrick any advice that he could recall, Wes considered it safe to join him on the bench.

"Beautiful day," Patrick observed.

"It's perfect," said Wes. Was this why he'd called him over? To talk about the weather? Wes wasn't complaining; he'd much rather talk about that than his failings as a librarian, but he suspected there was something else the cardigan clad octogenarian wanted to discuss.

"I'm wondering if I could get your advice," said Patrick.

Wes should've known. "Of course, but anything you may have heard about my skills as an advice giver hasn't been updated to include today's feedback. It hasn't been good." He filled Patrick in on today's debacles, but his companion just chuckled.

"That doesn't worry me. Folks around here could use some shaking up from time to time. Besides, you were doing your best, and that's all anyone can do. What other people do is up to them."

"That sounds like the advice I got from Ed over at the tavern." Maybe Wes was being a little hard on himself. He didn't tell Chloe to go all vampire hunter in real life, after all, and Emma was a woman who did what she was going to do, no matter what anyone else told her. She had gumption.

Wes admired that about her. It was what he admired about Bea, as well.

"Anyway, do you have a minute?" Patrick asked.

Wes didn't have anywhere to be for the rest of the day. "Sure. What's bothering you?"

"I bet you didn't know this about me, but I have a younger brother. Name's Leroy."

"No. I didn't know that? Does he live around here?"

"Not too far. He moved away for a while, but he's lived up in Ephraim since he retired twenty years ago. That's also about the time we stopped speaking to each other."

"Really?"

"You're surprised. I can tell. There's a part of me that's gratified to hear that, but you wouldn't have been surprised if you'd known me back when I was a younger man."

"What happened?"

Patrick sighed. "It's a long story, but I'll try to make it short. You wouldn't guess it to look at me, but I used to be quite an athlete. I played baseball, even went semi-pro for a couple of years before I blew out my knee. My brother was quiet; he was a skinny, sensitive kid. My parents didn't have any time for him. We all teased him. We acted like it was all in fun, but he was never the one doing the laughing. If he complained about how he was treated, his treatment got worse, and that included what he got from me."

Wes wished he couldn't imagine people being cruel like that because someone didn't fit in, but unfortunately, he'd experienced it first-hand. He'd been practically laughed out of town when it was revealed at the end of his senior year of high school that he still had imaginary friends.

He left town and didn't come back for over ten years. He'd found his way to forgiving the people who had rejected him and embracing the village, but he had a soft spot for those who marched to the beat of their own drum. Knowing the pain that such treatment could cause, he couldn't help but see Patrick in a slightly different light.

"He became a geography professor." Patrick wrung his hands. "We didn't talk much. I knew he harbored resentment. I understood why, but I never could bring myself to apologize. I was afraid to. I don't know what I thought would happen if I did, but the prospect terrified me. I guess I wanted to move on and pretend it didn't happen. The problem was, my parents didn't let up. We'd get together over the holidays and they'd still be bringing up some clumsy thing he did thirty years before. I sat idly by while all this was going on. I wasn't joining in anymore, but I wasn't about to stick my neck out either.

"When my parents died, everything came out. Leroy said he'd only been civil for their sake, and he was finished with me. He didn't even sound angry about it, just resigned. We haven't talked since their funeral. I got word that his wife passed away five years ago, and I lost the love of my life last fall. We're two old men, all alone, and maybe he still doesn't want anything to do with me, but I'm going to go up there and apologize anyway. He might laugh in my face, but I don't care anymore. It's what I should've done years ago, and that's time I'll never get back."

Patrick had said he wanted Wes's advice, but it seemed like he already knew what he wanted to do. "Where do I come in?" Wes asked.

"I have two requests. There's no reason for you to agree to either of them, other than to help out an old man, but I'm asking anyway. One: Will you help me with my apology? You probably don't remember me from when you were growing up, other than maybe as the village postman, but I remember you. I suspect you might know a thing or two about making amends."

Wes nodded. "And the second thing?"

"I'd like you to drive me to Ephraim to see my brother."

Chapter Fourteen

In Which a Shocking Letter Lands in Chloe's Mailbox

When Betsy got to work the day after Nick's accident, Chloe was still in her Rosie the Riveter pajamas, typing away once again. "I'm on a roll," she said. "Don't interrupt me."

Betsy was tempted to point out that she wasn't the one who did the vast majority of the interrupting around here, but she held back. Carefully sitting down in front of her computer in order to make a minimum amount of sound, Betsy checked her inbox. She still hadn't replied to Gadgetgal, and he'd need some cheering up today.

Nick had gone home after getting his stitches. There was no sign that he'd gotten a concussion, but he was in quite a bit of pain. Karl had taken off of work today in order to help out around the house.

Betsy planned to stop over there tonight to bring the whole family dinner from Emma's. Karl had tried to talk her out of it, saying he was happy to cook, but she wouldn't take no for an answer. She'd never seen his parents in at Emma's; it would be a huge treat for all of them.

Betsy tapped her fingers lightly over the keyboard, not sure what she wanted to say. Something was happening between her and Karl. She could feel it.

Did he?

Hi Gadgetgal, It's not too late for you either, and given your incredible skills as a time travelling zoologist, anyone would be lucky to end up with you, no matter the time or place. Is it daunting to have to choose a partner amongst everyone who has ever lived? Anyway, I'm starting to think we should meet in person so we can help each other find our perfect matches. Are you going to the fair on Saturday? I'll be there, wearing a purple dress and white sneakers. If you want to reveal your secret identity, meet me by the stage during the bachelor auction.

Betsy

She hit send. That was it. If Karl was interested in her, he'd meet her at the fair, and she'd tell him how she felt. If not, well, then she'd misread the situation terribly and would keep going on the same way she had been for the past year. Would she feel awful and let-down? Yes. But she and Karl would still be friends, no matter what. This was a chance she had to take. She was coming around to believing in herself. It felt good. She rested her hand on her belly and got to work.

Chloe didn't speak or move until lunch, when she ran out to grab the mail. She raced back in, her face red, her mouth opening and closing like she wanted to say something but couldn't bring herself to spit out the words. Sprinting over to the table, she threw a letter down in front of Betsy.

The return address was from someone whose name was unfamiliar. Why were they sending something to...*Orpheus Adair*? What on earth?

"Is this a joke?" Betsy asked. "Why would someone send you a letter with this name on it?

"Look at the address."

Oh. It wasn't Chloe's address. It was her neighbor's.

"I knew it," Chloe said. "I knew something weird was going on."

"But what does this mean? I thought you said his name was Noah something-or-other."

"Noah Clark. Right. That's who bought the house, but the person getting mail there shares a name with the vampire from the Nina Striker books. What are the chances of that?"

The chances were infinitesimal, but Betsy still didn't understand what the implications were. Was there really someone out there named Orpheus Adair? "This has to be a joke. Call Wes. If he didn't stick this in our mailbox this morning, I'll give up my rights as the winner of our bet."

"*If* you win, you mean."

"I already won. I know who it is. Or at least, I think I know. It's Karl."

"Are you sure?"

"No. I'm not one hundred percent positive, but I'll know by Saturday."

"Fine. I'm calling Wes, but I'm telling you,

there's something weird going on around here."

"Yes, you've been saying that." Betsy had to admit though, this was getting pretty strange.

Chloe grabbed her phone and called her prime suspect. "Wes?" She put him on speakerphone. "This is Betsy and Chloe. We got a strange letter in the mail today, and we're wondering if you had anything to do with it."

"Is this from the same person who's been sending you funny e-mails? It's still not me," Wes replied.

"I think he's telling the truth," Chloe whispered to Betsy. Betsy agreed. "We think we have the e-mails figured out, but now something's come up that's funny 'strange'."

"What is it?"

"It's a letter, addressed to my mysterious neighbor, under the name Orpheus Adair."

Wes was silent on the other end. "Are you joking?"

"No. I swear. Would I joke about something like this?"

Another round of silence. "Yes...but I believe you. Will you send me a picture?"

"Gladly."

"Who's it from?"

"There's no return address. Don't worry. I'm going to get to the bottom of this."

"I'm sure you will...but Chloe? Take 'er easy, okay?"

Chloe scoffed. "Of course I will. Think about who you're talking to."

Lots of silence on his end. "Done. And I still say take 'er easy."

Betsy laughed. Chloe shot her a dirty look. "Why does everyone always think I'm up to something?"

Neither Betsy nor Wes replied. After Chloe hung up, she got up and paced the length of the kitchen. "You know what this means, don't you?"

Betsy didn't.

Chloe stopped and stared her down. "This takes things to a whole new level."

"What are you going to do?"

"I haven't decided yet."

"You can't keep the letter, you know."

"I'm not going to." Chloe snapped a photo before heading for the door. "I'm putting it in his mailbox right now."

That was reassuring to hear.

"This isn't the end though," she added. "Not by a long shot."

That was less reassuring.

When Chloe returned from delivering the letter, still in her pink camo pajama pants and Rosie the Riveter t-shirt, she sat back down and got to work as if nothing had happened. She wouldn't forget about this, though. It was the calm before the storm. Betsy followed suit, getting ready to make a few calls. No need to stir the pot. Chloe would do that herself, in her own time.

"You gave up your win, remember," Chloe mumbled as she typed. She hadn't forgotten about that, either.

***

That night, in Karl's parents' living room, Betsy lounged in a worn but comfortable stuffed armchair. His whole family had been incredibly appreciative of the dinner and invited Betsy to stay afterwards. She'd agreed, with the understanding that they would go on with their night as if she wasn't there. Betsy didn't want them to fuss.

If possible, Nick looked even worse than he had the day before. His bruises had turned nasty shades of yellow, green, and brown. Having eaten his favorite BLT (Emma had made an exception and dug some bacon out of the freezer just for him), he reclined on the couch, his legs covered with a sheet and his head propped up on a couple of throw pillows. He and his dad watched a superhero movie while Betsy pretended to be paying attention. She caught Karl doing the same thing. She stole a glance at him then looked away when their eyes met.

Finally, Karl whispered, "Want to go outside so we can talk?"

"I'd love to," Betsy replied.

Nick sushed them. They got up and sneaked away.

Would Karl admit that he was the one who'd been sending the e-mails? If he did, should Betsy say anything about her feelings for him? She'd planned to tell him at the fair, but maybe doing it now would be even better. They'd be alone, and if everything went off the rails and she made a fool of herself, she wouldn't be stuck at a big celebration.

Stepping outside, Karl shut the front door behind them. They sat down together on the porch swing. "That's better," he said. "I never understood the appeal of those superhero movies."

"Me either," Betsy agreed, resting her head on his shoulder like she used to when they were kids. "You loved Spiderman though."

"I loved the comics. Remember how in love you were with Nikola Tesla?"

"Remember? I still am."

"Wow. I had no idea. I never mustered up the courage to ask you how that came about."

"Do you really have to? It was Chloe. She got me a big poster of him for my birthday one year. I had no idea who he was, but I fell hopelessly in love with him. Maybe it was those dark piercing eyes or the thick mustache."

"So you have a thing for facial hair?" Karl asked, teasing her.

"Totally," she said, as if she was also joking like a normal person and not at all tempted to reach up and stroke his bearded square jawed face. He smelled like he always did, with that added touch of Bea's citrus lotion.

She sat up straight and scooted over, putting a bit of space between them.

"Did you move the poster from your bedroom when you moved into your new house?" Karl asked.

"No. It was getting a little curled at the edges. I couldn't bear to throw him out, though. I gave it to Goodwill. They probably got rid of it, but I like to imagine there's someone out there who's enjoying Tesla nearly as much as I did."

"I don't know if that's possible, but I hope so too."

"What about you?" Betsy asked. "I couldn't have been the only one to have spent my teen years pining after some silly crush. Chloe didn't get you a Marie Curie poster, did she?"

Karl suddenly became very interested in the tall oak tree in front of his parents' house. A tire swing used to hang there. When had they taken it down? She and Karl used to push each other on it, and Karl swore he'd once gone so high that he'd spun all the way around the branch. Karl and Nick were too old for it now, obviously. Betsy laughed, picturing the two strapping men pushing each other on the rubbery black tire.

"I bet my dad missed you at the shop today," she said.

Karl rubbed the back of his neck like he always did when he was nervous. Was there something going on at the shop? Betsy had been worried when Karl started there. She didn't know what she'd do if her dad fired him for some silly reason, but now that he'd been a fixture for a while, she thought he was secure. The one thing her dad disliked nearly as much as a chatty mechanic was change.

"He seemed fine with me taking a day off. It's

hard to tell."

"Yeah. He's a man of few words, but he must like you. You're over the one year mark. That's a record."

"So, have you figured out the identity of your mystery reviewer?" Karl asked, changing the subject.

"I need to confirm with him first, but I think I have."

"I think you have too, but he has to tell you something."

"Oh?" Betsy tensed. If he was about to make a big declaration of love, she wanted to remember it forever, but she was so full of anticipation that she couldn't focus.

"He can't meet you off stage during...You know it's me, right? I feel weird talking like this."

She laughed and the spell was broken.

"You can't meet me during the bachelor auction?" she asked. "I thought it would be funny to watch. There's a mystery contestant..." *Oh no.* He didn't have to say it, and she didn't want him to. "You're the mystery contestant, aren't you?"

He nodded then looked at her beseechingly, as if asking for forgiveness. "Chloe roped me into it. It sounded like a good cause, and I thought it might be fun. Like you said, it's funny, but I don't really want to do it anymore."

Betsy wrenched her eyes open wide and grinned. Looking happy about this was painful. Karl would be going on a date with someone else at the exact moment she thought there was finally a chance they would be together? It was like smiling through a tetanus shot. "You should totally do it. I agree. It'll be so funny."

"I thought you might be disappointed."

"Me? No way. I love it. You'll be in demand. We can meet up afterwards and talk about your date. I wonder if it'll be someone we know." What was she doing? She still had a chance here. She could tell him how she felt. What if this was her *last* chance? But what if this was his opportunity to find someone... someone better for him. Someone less pregnant with another man's baby, perhaps.

"I'll meet up with you right after the auction," Karl said. "We can try our luck at plunging Chloe or Arthur into the dunk tank."

"Sounds perfect." Betsy did her level best to sound chipper. "I better run. Say goodbye to your family for me. Nick was really into his movie. I don't want to interrupt him."

"Are you sure? It's not that late. We could take a walk or something."

He could have no idea how tempted she was to stay, but her resolve to let him go was weakening as they spoke. "It's a good idea, and normally I would, but I've had some long days. I get a lot more tired than I used to."

"You're growing a person," he said, putting his hand on her belly. He slid it away. "Sorry, you probably hate when people do that."

Not this person, Betsy thought. She guided his hand back to the curve of her upper stomach. "She's kicking right now. Well, she kicks all the time, but she's really active. Maybe she recognizes your voice."

She felt another kick, right where Karl's hand pressed against the fabric of her dress. "Did you feel that?" she asked.

"I did. That's incredible. I'm so happy for you. I know this isn't how you pictured it going, but you're already an amazing mom."

Betsy smiled at him, for real this time. If anyone knew how much hearing that meant to her, that person would be Karl. She felt a lump rising in her throat; she pushed it down with a gulp.

"I'll let you get moving," said Karl, patting her on the leg and standing. "I'm going to help my mom in the kitchen. She bought some ice cream for Nick on her way home. Are you sure you don't want to stay?"

"Thank you, but I'm going to go home, take a bath, and climb into bed."

"Good plan. See you Saturday?"

"See you."

As Betsy pulled out of the long dirt driveway that led from his parents' little white farmhouse, she looked back at the porch. Karl had already gone back inside.

***

The rest of the week passed with no more messages from Gadgetgal. Chloe didn't mention the letter again either, although Betsy had no doubt she was still scheming. At the end of the day on Friday, Chloe and Betsy drove over to their parents' house in Old

Blue.

"Karl told me he's the mystery bachelor," Betsy informed Chloe.

"What? He wasn't supposed to tell anyone. Keep it a secret, okay?"

"I will. I kind of forced it out of him. I asked him if he wanted to watch it with me, and it would've been hard to do that from up on stage."

"I'm so excited about the guys who agreed to do it. They're all going to be in demand. I wouldn't have even considered Karl, because he's *Karl*, my little sister's friend who always followed us around, but he's grown up. I know you haven't noticed, but I've been hearing whispers around town."

Betsy's heart sank. "I've noticed," she said quietly.

Chloe slammed on the brakes. "What a minute. *What*? He's been in love with you since you were kids. Don't tell me you're falling for him."

Betsy looked at Chloe without turning her head and smiled ruefully.

"No way," said Chloe. "And here I am trying to set him up. I'm so sorry. I had no idea. None at all."

"I know you didn't. I didn't either. It hit me out of nowhere, and I haven't been able to shake it."

"Why don't you tell him? Heck, I'll tell him if you don't."

"Please don't. Nothing's been easy for him, and I'm..." She spread her arms, exposing her belly. "He can find someone less encumbered."

"He doesn't want someone less encumbered.

He wants you."

"I'm not like you. You do some crazy stuff, but your heart's in the right place."

"And yours isn't?"

"It is now. It wasn't before, and I have to live with the consequences. Karl doesn't."

Chloe shook her head as she carried on down the road. Betsy could practically hear her scheming, but neither of them said more about Karl or anything else all the way to their childhood home. When they arrived, their mom ran out of the kitchen in a wraparound black dress, her blonde hair snipped into a sleek bob. Her eyebrows had been freshly penciled into perfect light brown arches and thin gold earrings dangled to just above her collar bone.

"My girls!" she shrieked. "I wish Hannah could be here. She's too uncomfortable to drive long distances anymore, but I'm thrilled to see the two of you."

"I believe it," said Betsy. Their older sister Hannah was due in a week, which was two weeks earlier than Betsy's due date.

Their mom shuttled them through the foyer and into the kitchen, where a feast was already laid out on the kitchen table. "It's like Thanksgiving dinner in here," Chloe said, lifting the lid on a platter to reveal a steaming tray of cheesy potatoes. They smelled incredible.

"Where's Dad?" Betsy asked.

"He's in the den. He wanted to talk to you before we ate." She lowered her voice. "He's been crabby this week, so tread carefully."

He wanted to talk to her? Betsy hoped he hadn't found out about her brakes. It wouldn't be the end of the world, but she'd rather be able to maintain some veneer of responsibility for a change.

"Hurry up," Chloe begged her. "I'm not going to be able to hold off on eating these."

Betsy scurried away and found her dad on the sofa in the den. He was watching golf, but he turned it off when she came into the room. She sat down on the recliner kitty corner from him and put the feet up. She finally understood the appeal of these things. They were ugly, but this was the most comfortable she'd been in weeks.

"You wanted to see me?" she asked.

He cut to the chase. "It's Karl. I'm going to have to let him go. I know you're close, and I'm sorry about his brother's accident, but he lied to me. I'm not comfortable keeping him on."

"He lied to you?" Betsy snapped her feet back down to sit up straight. "That doesn't sound like Karl."

"I'm just as surprised as you are."

"What happened?"

"I'd rather not say. I'll give him a good reference, but I'm going to fire him first thing Monday morning."

Chapter Fifteen

In Which Karl Reluctantly Competes

At Chloe's request, Karl arrived at the fair early Saturday morning. He found Arthur perched on the bench above the dunk tank, wearing swim trunks and staring down into the clear still water.

"You sure you want to do this?" Karl asked.

Arthur looked up with a start. He'd been so intent on contemplating his doom that he must not have heard Karl's approach. "I said I would, but now I'm not so sure. It's one thing to jump in, but to sit here and wait, not knowing when my seat will disappear beneath me...But hey, it's better than having to be in the bachelor auction."

Karl laughed. "I guess neither of us anticipated the power of Chloe's persuasive efforts."

"I was already very familiar with them..." Arthur gave an exaggerated shudder, but his accompanying smile let Karl know he didn't mind having to go along with Chloe's schemes.

"Can I ask you something?"

"Go ahead. I'm stuck above a cube of water."

"Are George and Betsy dating? I haven't come out and asked her, because I thought it might be touchy if they're not. I hope you don't mind me asking."

"It's fine. I get it, and it's a tough situation. And to answer your question: no. He broke up with her last fall and that was that. I probably don't need to tell you this, but George isn't much of one for commitment."

Karl did get that impression. As he'd suspected, this was a case of George not wanting anyone else to have Betsy, but also not being up for the work of a real relationship.

"You're a great friend to her," Arthur added. "Chloe talks about you a lot, about how much she appreciates you looking out for Betsy."

"I'm the lucky one," said Karl. He looked around. No one else was outside. They must be getting ready in the barn. He'd better find Chloe and figure out what he was supposed to be doing. Should he have prepared something to say? Chloe had told him his job was to 'pose up there', but surely the women would want to hear him speak? Then again, maybe not.

Waving goodbye to Arthur, Karl headed inside the barn, where Grace and Betsy were tying colorful balloons to an arch. "Coming through." Chloe peeked out from behind a red and gold vintage popcorn machine, wheeling it past Karl and parking it by the entrance.

Coming to a stop, she raced around the machine and gave Karl an appraising once-over. "You're here!"

"Did you think there was a chance I wouldn't

show?"

"I predicted that at least one of you three would pull a runner, but maybe you'll all prove me wrong."

"Well, it is a charity auction..."

"You look perfect. I love the jeans and t-shirt look for you. I'm billing you as a rugged mechanic with a heart of gold."

"What should I do up there?"

"Just look pretty."

"I'll do my best." Karl laughed. Out of the corner of his eye, he could see that Betsy had stopped tying balloons and stood still, listening in on their conversation. "This is just a silly thing. I'm not taking it seriously at all."

"Yeah. Me either," said Chloe, following his gaze and raising her voice a bit obviously. "It's not like you're looking for a relationship. It'll be one date. It's not even a date. It's a charity get-together."

"Exactly. It's all in the name of helping you guys out."

"The women I talked to are looking at it that way too. It's just a goofy event. Nobody's looking to get married or anything."

"Definitely not. Can I help out around here?"

Chloe directed Karl back outside, where he dragged a kiddy pool out of the garage and filled it with water from the garden hose. A basket of rubber ducks with different colored spots on them was nestled beneath the back porch. Soon the ducks bobbed in the water, nearly filling the pool. Kids could choose a duck and would win prizes depending on the color they revealed.

Karl made himself useful for another half hour, never running into Betsy again. Was she avoiding him? The finishing touches had just been completed when people started arriving in droves. Chloe really had promoted this event all over the place. There were quite a few people here that Karl had never seen before; a lot of them looked like summer tourists, who usually didn't come to this kind of thing.

Karl mingled a bit then found Wes. He was twisting up an elaborate balloon dragon for an awe-struck group of boys. Karl alternated between goofing around at the balloon station and helping Grace with the duck pool until it was almost time for the bachelor auction.

Betsy was on the far side of the barn, sitting at a table and chatting with some friends. He'd planned to talk to her before the auction, but Chloe summoned him before he had a chance. He climbed the stage, joined by Lucas and Jack, who looked almost as nervous as he felt.

"First time in the Door County bachelor circuit?" Lucas asked. With his fitted, flat front shorts, button down shirt, and breezy light blue blazer with matching boat shoes, he cut a very different figure from Karl. In Karl's defense, though, he'd gone with a t-shirt with a front pocket and chest stripe, which was a bit of an improvement over his solid gray or green staples.

"I've been around the block a few times," Karl

responded.

"Really? Is this something they do often around here?"

"No. I'm messing with you. I have no idea what to expect."

Jack, who was looking pale, said, "Do you think they'll notice if I slip out the back?"

"It'll be fine," said Karl. "Betsy assured me no one was taking this..."

A loud whoop cut through the excited murmurs of the crowd as Chloe strutted onto the stage. "Welcome to the first annual Men of Namur bachelor auction!"

Cheers and catcalls erupted from the crowd.

"I know you're all excited to meet our bachelors, but before you do, I want to remind everyone that all the proceeds from the auction will be going towards a fund we've established to hire a veteran who's interested in the field of agriculture."

This announcement was met with even more enthusiastic cheering. "Let's start with Lucas." Chloe pulled a note card out of her pocket and read aloud. "He's a transplant from Chicago who enjoys kayaking, old home restoration, and long walks on the beach. He encourages anyone with carpentry skills to bet high." Everyone laughed as Lucas stepped forward. A couple of the women jumped out of their seats and started calling out bids.

"Hold on, ladies," Chloe said, motioning for them to sit down. "What do you think this is? A barn?" She chuckled. "Because it is, get it?" Crickets.

"Anyway, raise your hand if you want to make a bid. We're going to start the bidding at twenty dollars. Do I hear twenty?" One of the women from the bachelorette group that was staying at the inn raised her hand. "Alright, we've got twenty, do I hear thirty? Thirty?"

Hands flew up left and right. By the time the bidding had wound down, Lucas had brought in $190, securing a date with the persistent lodger who had made the first bid.

"That wasn't so bad," he said, exiting stage right and leaving Jack and Karl alone on stage. Karl hoped he wouldn't be going next. He wasn't sure if Jack would be able to stand the pressure of being up here all alone.

"Next up is our surprise bachelor, Karl."

"Sorry, man," Karl said, patting Jack on the shoulder. "You'll be fine." Jack gulped and nodded stiffly while Karl stepped up next to Chloe.

"Karl is a mechanic at the best shop in Door County." Chloe got a whoop from her mom for that one. Her dad rubbed his head in the corner of the barn. Karl hadn't noticed him in the crowd until now. It disconcerted him to have his boss here, not only because this was kind of embarrassing, which it was, but because of the chill that had persisted between them when Karl went back to work at the end of the week.

"He likes to watch football, run, cook, and hang out with his little brother." That last bit garnered a couple of sighs from the crowd. "Same deal. We're starting at twenty dollars."

Immediately, a few hands flew up. The bidding

went on and on until two women, one Karl recognized and one he didn't know at all, were the lone competitors. They raised the bid again and again, glaring at each other. Karl started getting nervous. What happened to not taking this too seriously? Eventually, one of the bidders backed down, and the winner, a stunning woman with caramel brown hair, pumped her fist in victory while the other clapped good-naturedly for appearances but maintained a sneer.

He'd gone for $240.

He scanned the crowd, looking for Betsy. She wasn't in the barn. Maybe she was outside, trying to dunk Arthur with Grace. Once he'd fallen in a couple of times, Arthur was totally into it, taunting people to try their luck.

When Karl got outside though, Betsy's car was gone. He pulled out his phone and sent her a text. *Did you leave? Was hoping to split cotton candy.*

She responded right away. *I went home. Tired.*

Stay there, he wrote back. *Coming over with food.*

Don't. Stay and have fun. How was the auction?

Fine. No fun without you. Be there soon.

Okay, but I'm being boring.

Karl ran through the fair, grabbing up a bag of popcorn, another of cotton candy, and a swirly multicolored sucker. He hadn't counted on Betsy leaving, but other than that, phase one of his plan had been a success.

Time to kick off phase two.

Chapter Sixteen

In Which Wes Uncovers an Unappetizing Treat

The fair had wrapped up, and Wes was stowing away his supply of extra balloons into a canvas bag, when Bea sidled up next to him.

"Here it is," she said, "the site of our wedding reception. Can you believe it's only a week away?"

Wes couldn't. When he'd proposed on New Year's Eve, June had seemed like it would never come, and now here they were, nearly ready to become husband and wife. Well, she was ready. He was almost ready. If only he could be certain he wasn't going to mess it up. "I can't wait," he said.

"We're still planning on meeting with Lindsay and Grace tomorrow to discuss the details of our reception, right?"

"You wanted me there, too? I thought you were doing that."

Bea's face fell. Wes felt terrible, but he'd truly thought, when they'd discussed it last month, that Bea was going to be the one finalizing their plans. "No," she said. "We're supposed to do it together. I want it to be a reflection of both of us."

"I thought most of the details were already ironed out."

"They are, but they were going to go over everything we've chosen: the décor, flowers, things like that, and make sure we like how they go together. They have quite a lot of supplies on hand to add if we want to make any changes."

Wes picked up his bag of balloons, and he and Bea headed inside to see if Lindsay and Grace needed any help cleaning up. When they got inside, Wes didn't even bother to ask. It looked like a circus had exploded inside the barn. A bunch of balloons had broken free and were drifting across the floor. Soda, popcorn, and cotton candy, punctuated with pieces of straw that had sprung free from the straw bale seating, littered every corner of the building.

"I wish I could be there," he said, grabbing a broom while Bea took up a dustpan. "But I promised Patrick I'd drive him somewhere tomorrow."

"Patrick?" Bea asked. "Chloe's neighbor?"

Wes nodded. "He has a younger brother who lives up north, and they haven't seen each other for ages. He doesn't drive anymore, so I agreed to take him up to Ephraim."

"So you won't be there tomorrow?"

"If you really want me to, I'd be fine with rescheduling, but it's pretty important to him."

"This is pretty important to me," said Bea. She sighed. "But I understand. You should go with Patrick. It's nice of you, and it should be no problem for me to finalize our plans." He heard what she was saying, but the look on her face hadn't changed from one of disappointed resignation.

Wes didn't want to let Bea down, but Patrick had finally mustered up the courage to face his brother, and Wes was reluctant to make him wait any longer. What if he lost his nerve? "Thanks for understanding," he said, trying and failing to sweep a chunk of pink cotton candy into Bea's waiting dustpan. It stuck to the broom. "It's going to be a beautiful day for us no matter what you choose."

Bea didn't respond as she headed back out the door.

As tempted as Wes felt to follow Bea and tell her he'd changed his mind, that he'd be there to put the finishing touches on their wedding plans, he was rooted to the spot. He stood there, holding his broom. This trip with Patrick, for some reason Wes couldn't explain to anyone else, let alone himself, felt significant.

He promised himself, and made a silent promise to Bea as well, that if this final adventure ended in a reconciliation between Patrick and his brother, Wes would give up feeling like a fraud and have the confidence he needed to be a husband, a son-in-law and, eventually, a father.

This wasn't the World Naked Bike Ride anymore.

It was time to man up.

***

When Wes pulled up to Patrick's house the following morning, the kindly-looking old man was waiting for him on the front porch with a shiny thermos in one hand and a paper bag in the other. He bounded down the stairs with surprising ease and whipped opened the passenger door.

"Well, here we are," Patrick said, "a couple of guys on a road trip. I haven't done anything like this in ages."

"It's been a while for me, too," said Wes.

"I hear your fair was quite a hit. Chloe stopped over last night with some leftover popcorn and gummy bears. I didn't have the heart to tell her I can't eat them, so I brought some along for you."

"Hey, thanks. It was fun." Wes pulled onto Patrick's tree-lined street, passing Chloe's on the way. "They raised quite a bit of money for the Demeter Society. I don't know if I told you, but I'm getting married next Saturday, and we're having our reception at the barn."

"I may have heard a little bit about that. You're marrying the Delcroix girl, aren't you?"

"I am."

"Big farm they've got. I'm quite a bit older than her parents, but I used to go over there sometimes to help her grandparents with the harvest in the fall. They always had the biggest pumpkins. It's a miracle how some of those houses have stayed in the same family all these years. I never would've expected it. So many young people move away these days."

"Like me. I left for a while, but I've come to appreciate small town life."

"I left for a while too, but a certain young woman drew me right back. Sound familiar?" Patrick chuckled.

"Very."

Wes turned onto the highway, and they made their way north, heading for Ephraim. Before he'd picked up Patrick, Wes was nervous that they'd run out of things to talk about, that driving with someone he barely knew for over an hour would become awkward by mile five.

As it turned out, however, his worries were unfounded. Patrick told Wes stories about the old general store on Main Street, which had become the Namur Public Library before it was demolished late last year. As they drove on, he also talked more about his life growing up. It wasn't all serious, but he and his brother had certainly been at odds about a lot of things, so much so that it was difficult for Wes not to laugh about some of their disputes.

Patrick picked up on Wes's discomfort after the first suppressed laugh, and said, "I know. It sounds absolutely foolish now, but you know how it is when you're right in the middle of something, and you can't get out of your own way? I just couldn't help but rankle him."

Wes could certainly relate to the sensation of being unable to get out of his own way. It was a tricky thing to accomplish.

"We were in competition with each other and on edge all the time. There's one dispute I'll never forget: there was this couch in the basement. I swore it was green. My brother was equally convinced it was blue. We ended up having to call it the "downstairs couch" because any other descriptor would launch us into a fight all over again. I did call it green every now and then, though, just to get his goat.

"Maybe it was a way for you to get out some of your anger at each other, without having to talk about the real stuff," said Wes.

"See? You know what you're talking about."

"Sometimes I do, but I haven't been that great at helping people out lately. It makes me nervous about getting married." Why was Wes telling this man, someone he hardly knew, about his biggest insecurity? He couldn't take it back now, but he was embarrassed. He'd never admitted that to anyone.

Was Wes becoming like his patrons, keeping someone captive in the mobile library and baring his soul? Maybe there was something about this bus that shook loose buried secrets.

"Nervous about getting married? I don't know you well, but if I can do it, I'm certain you can. You're smarter than you give yourself credit for."

"Or maybe I'm less smart than I give myself credit for. I have a wild imagination; I'll give myself that, and I love to read. I know a lot of big words, so I'm amazing at Scrabble, but when it comes to people...How can I handle the tough things that life throws at a person? I don't know if I'm someone who should be entrusted with serious things."

"You already are, though, whether you want to be or not. I think it may be the price you pay for having other people in your life. What's the other option?"

Patrick didn't wait for an answer.

"Look at me. I didn't want to be responsible for my brother, and to a great extent I'm not, right? But I *am* responsible for how I treat him, as his brother, and instead I acted like a fool. Do you want to know what I see when I look at you?"

"I'm not sure...I suppose that depends on what it is."

"I see a guy who treats people like they're important, like they deserve to be listened to. Look at what you're doing today, look at what you've been doing nearly every day as the librarian of this town. You're listening to people, giving them a place to be heard and valued. Not only that, you're trying to be helpful. That's a lot more than I did for a good chunk of my life. I don't know you well, but you seem capable of doing a whole lot of important things."

"Thanks, Patrick. I needed that." It wasn't like he was going to turn around and become perfectly confident overnight, but a little extra boost of courage goes a long way.

"Of course. I'm the one who should be thanking you. I wasn't sure if you'd agree to this harebrained scheme when I suggested it, but I sure do appreciate it."

Swooping around a tight curve in the highway, they reached a scenic overlook. Eddies of dark and light swirled in the otherwise calm water of Green Bay. The village of Fish Creek, with its jumble of quaint shops, beachfront restaurants, and busy marinas lay straight ahead.

“I hope you don’t mind,” said Patrick, “but I could use the facilities any time you come upon a convenient spot.

“Of course. I’ll stop right up here.” Wes pulled up in front of a low white building with a covered porch that housed a collection of shops.

Patrick left Wes alone in the bus with the bag of gummy bears. Wes, who hadn’t eaten breakfast that morning, looked longingly at the brown paper sack. It wasn’t the healthiest choice, but he’d just have one or two. He unrolled the bag and peeked inside, envisioning a muddle of jewel bright gummies.

What *was* that?

What ever it was, it had nothing to do with gummy bears. Wes was in the middle of a road trip with a man who’d brought along a bag of something lumpy, brown, and decidedly inedible. He rolled the top back up and, putting the bag back exactly as he’d found it, stared straight ahead. Patrick was back in the car a minute later, ready to hit the road and go… wherever it was they were going.

Chapter Seventeen

In Which One Happy Surprise Leads to Another

Back in Namur, Betsy paced behind her front door, waiting for Karl to pick her up for their first date. He wouldn't tell her what they were going to do, but he did give her instructions to dress comfortably and plan to be out all day. She'd gone a little more on the cute than the comfortable side, but who could blame her? It was Betsy's first date with her favorite person.

She couldn't believe it when Karl had stopped by after the fair. She'd already put on her pajamas, wanting the day to be over already. It was supposed to be a fun day. It was a fair, after all, but the thought of someone else on a date with Karl devastated her in ways she hadn't expected. Betsy had stayed long enough to see Lucas walk off stage before she trudged to her car and drove straight home.

The fact that she knew she wasn't good for Karl, that she'd only make his life difficult, made it a thousand times worse. Somewhere back there in that hollering crowd, there was some sweet simple woman who would make Karl happier than Betsy ever could. Betsy, with her old car, her string of emotionally detached boyfriends, and her unbelievable ability to have missed the perfect guy who was in front of her all along, didn't even deserve to be feeling sorry for herself, but here she was.

She still didn't suspect anything when Karl showed up with the food. She'd changed back out of her pajamas, but she wasn't really hungry. It was all she could do to keep it together when she asked Karl who had won him at the auction. They were curled up on the couch, picking at a fluffy clump of cotton candy.

"Some woman I met at the fair. Her name's Sophie."

"So, when's the big date?" Betsy asked. It came out as a high-pitched squeak.

Karl stretched, satisfied and cat-like, and Betsy's stomach gave a lurch. "Oh, we're not going on one. I wanted to tell you before the auction without letting Chloe know the game was rigged, but I couldn't find you. I paid her to bid on me. I didn't expect the bidding to go as high as it did, but it was worth it. I was acting on someone else's behalf."

"What do you mean? Whose?"

"Yours."

She looked back at him with a glazed look. Maybe she hadn't heard him right. "Mine? What do you mean?"

Karl shot her a huge, hopeful smile. "I wanted to go on a date with you, and I'm sorry to be so bold, but it seemed like you wanted to go on a date with me. It wouldn't be right to make you pay for our first date, so I bought it myself, through someone else, for you.

For me, too."

"You bought a date for us?" Was this really happening? Perhaps Betsy had fallen asleep on the couch, and this was some kind of wonderful dream. She gave herself a little surreptitious pinch on the arm. Ouch! Yep. It was really happening.

"Are you mad?" Karl asked.

She shook her head. *No, just pinching myself.* "I'm not mad. I'm nervous."

"Afraid you're going to fall madly in love with me?"

He was joking, but little did he know how close he was coming to the truth. It had happened little by little, so that, by the time Betsy had recognized how things had changed between them, she was already so far gone there was no turning back. "I'm not afraid of...of that. I'm afraid of making your life more complicated than I already have."

"What do you mean?"

"I know about what happened at the shop with my dad. Why didn't you tell him you were helping me?"

"You asked me not to tell anyone."

"I know. I appreciate your loyalty, but I don't want you in trouble because of me. I admitted it was my car."

"What did he say?"

"About as much as he always does. It was something like, 'Huh. Not what I expected.'"

"That's...uninformative, but you didn't have to do that."

"Yes, I did. I almost cost you your job."

"How's that?"

Betsy squeezed her eyes shut then stared down at her feet. "I asked you to fix my car instead of going to my dad, and then you covered for me instead of protecting yourself. He thought you were up to something. Also, on the complication front, I'm really very pregnant."

"What? Why didn't you say something before?"

"I was hoping you wouldn't notice."

"Well, despite your low opinion of my observational skills, I did notice. I also *chose* to fix your car. It's not like you forced me into it. If you don't want to go on the date, that's totally fine, really, but only if it's because you're not interested in me like that. If you are though, then I get to decide what kinds of complications I invite into my life, and you just happen to be one I'm especially interested in."

"But..."

"Also, I don't know if *you've* noticed, but I have more than a couple complications of my own. Don't think you get to have the monopoly on difficulties around here. And don't think you haven't made everything that's ever happened to me a thousand times easier than it would've been without you."

Betsy's objections were melting away. That was incredibly sweet, but she hadn't done anything special. She loved spending time with Karl and his family. Was she being selfish in wanting to be with him? Maybe a little, but it didn't feel like selfishness when she looked into the eyes of the handsome, sweet, funny, blue-eyed mechanic on the couch next to her. "Are you sure?"

"Would you cut it out? You don't see yourself the way I do, but I wish you would. You're beautiful and kind. You're also too hard on yourself."

"If you're sure you want to do this. I mean, you know what you're getting into."

Karl laughed. "We did just meet…almost thirty years ago."

"Very funny. You know I'm being serious."

"So am I."

For all her hesitation, Betsy couldn't deny the expansive feeling that spread across her chest as she said, "Then yes. I would absolutely love to go on a date with you."

"Yes!" Karl yelled. "I mean, yeah. That should work for me too." He quit trying to play it cool and asked, "Are you free tomorrow?"

"Wow. You're not one to take things slow, are you?"

His lips spread into a smile. "Sometimes I am, but not right now."

Yikes. She was a goner.

"In that case, I'm intrigued and very free tomorrow."

"Pick you up at nine?"

"Make it nine thirty and you have a deal."

"It's a date, then."

"Yes, it is."

They sat there on the couch, with their sticky cotton candy fingertips and their goofy smiles until

Betsy took his hands in hers, leaned in close, and kissed him, ever so softly. Karl slid his hands from her grip, running them along either side of her waist and down to the small of her back. Betsy, leaning in closer, took an almost involuntary gasp as her gaze wandered from his eyes down to his slightly parted lips and back up again.

Hello, Karl.

Goodbye, whatever reason this had seemed like a bad idea.

Their noses skimmed as he dragged his warm breath across her lower lip. A hum of satisfaction pulsed through her. She wanted him. She'd waited for so long. Gripping a handful of his shirt, Betsy closed the gap between them and sank her mouth into his. He tasted like spun sugar and buttered popcorn, sweet and salty and something better, something more.

If their actual date was anything like its prelude, Betsy was in for a day to remember.

***

"Are you going to tell me where we're going?" Betsy asked from the front seat of Karl's truck. They'd already passed Egg Harbor and Fish Creek and were heading into Sister Bay.

"Not a chance. This is a super surprise date."

"Because you know I love surprises."

"I do know that, and I'm an expert on other things you love too, like..."

Rounding a bend in the highway, Al Johnson's Swedish Restaurant came into view. Betsy couldn't have been the only person whose mouth watered at the sight of the low, brown painted log cabin. The goats were out on the sod roof, too.

"Welcome to Swedish Pancakes topped with lingonberries and whipped cream," Karl announced.

"And hot chocolate with a tower of whipped cream taller than the mug. You're my hero. This is the best date ever."

"It's hasn't even started. Give me a chance to really wow you before you decide."

"Fine, but honestly, we could just drive around and I'd be happy. I love being with you."

"I love being with you, too. I always have," he said simply.

She stretched over and kissed him on the cheek. "Just so you know, Swedish Pancakes were on my summer bucket list, and I was sure it wasn't going to happen."

"You have a summer bucket list? Now that, I didn't know."

"It's a thing I'm doing this year. I'm determined to have new kinds of adventures."

"What else is on it?" Karl parked the car in the lot and turned to her with smiling eyes.

"Well, having a baby, obviously, and doing fun things with her."

"She'll be very portable. We can wear her and go on hikes."

"Yes! I would love that. I bet she will too." Betsy

continued ticking items off on her fingers. "Hiking was another one of the things I wanted to do-hiking The Ridges. I want to have a picnic at Whitefish Dunes, pick cherries, get ice cream at Wilson's, and eat pizza at Wild Tomato."

"So, lots of food related items?"

"Yes. Tons of them."

"Let's do it all. You might be surprised by how many we can accomplish today."

Karl got out of the truck and opened Betsy's door. They took a selfie with the goats before heading inside. The restaurant was hopping, but Karl had made a reservation. At a round table, on adorable wooden chairs with hearts carved into them, Betsy and Karl sat down and ordered without bothering to glance at the menu.

"I think you might need to start adding some new things to the list," said Karl as he lifted a glass filled with his own personal favorite-ice water-and took a drink.

Betsy could think of several things she'd like to add, all of them involving Karl. Her cheeks grew warm.

"You're getting that pregnancy flush again," said Karl. "Is it kind of annoying?"

It was time to confess. "It's not really a pregnancy flush. Well, maybe it's that too. I don't know, but it's mostly a Karl flush."

"You're kidding." He gave her one of his faux-smug knowing looks.

"You know I'm not. Did you really not notice?"

"Okay, fine, I thought it might be me. I just wanted to hear you say it. Once I did notice, it seemed incredible that I hadn't, but I really didn't. Not at first, anyway. It was Nick who pointed it out."

"We have Nick to thank for today?"

"I'd say so."

"How's he doing?"

"He was looking much better this morning. He's moving around a lot more too. He and my dad are keeping each other company."

Betsy wasn't sure if she should ask about his dad, but he'd seemed so quiet when they were over at his parents'. After the accident, his dad had some very dark times but, until she saw him the other day, Betsy would've said he was nearly back to being the funny, enthusiastic guy he'd been when they were kids.

Karl, squishing the end of his straw with his fingers, brought it up before she had a chance. "I'm worried about my dad. He's not up for doing anything. I think it might have something to do with Nick moving away for college. He wants him to go, but those two were best buddies. It'll be so quiet when he's gone." He lowered his voice and looked down at the table. "I'm pretty sure Nick's the only reason he's still here at all."

Heaviness settled over Betsy's heart. The years following his dad's accident had been particularly difficult for Karl. He hadn't even attended their high school graduation; he was at home with Nick. His mom was beside herself with worry. She took her husband from one appointment to another and encouraged him through his physical therapy while working as much as she could to keep them afloat. She leaned heavily on Karl.

"I'd like to visit them more often," said Betsy. "Maybe we can have a standing date and make dinner for them every Sunday night, if they'd like that."

"I'm certain they'd love that."

"In fact, why don't we go over there tonight? We can kick off the tradition."

"What about our date?" Karl looked surprised, but she could tell he was pleased as well.

"We have the rest of the day. Let's do whatever wonderful adventures you have planned until late afternoon, and then make dinner at their house. I haven't had your stir fry in forever."

"You know what? I haven't made stir fry in forever. You're right. Let's do it. I should tell you though; you're missing out on Wild Tomato pizza."

Betsy waved away the prospect of cheesy basil studded deliciousness without a second thought. "It'll be there all summer. Besides, I'm about to eat a ridiculous amount of whipped cream."

Chapter Eighteen

In Which a Display of Excitement is Avoided

The following morning was Monday. Karl never understood people's dislike of Mondays. It was the start of another week, another chance to begin anew and hope you learned a little something from the week before. Between his date with Betsy yesterday and their visit on the couch the day before that, he'd learned enough in the past week to last him the rest of the year, so he had that going for him.

His date with Betsy had gone even better than he could have imagined. It was like nothing had changed, but at the same time, everything had. They walked along the beach, ate giant waffle cones full of creamy custard, and listened to a band at Harbor View Park.

When they got to his parents' house around five, his whole family hid out in the living room to give Betsy and Karl some space, peeking into the kitchen every now and then to see how things were coming along. They were all so obviously thrilled for him that it would've been embarrassing with anyone else. As it was, he and Betsy glided around each other as they chopped, sautéed, and boiled. They also laughed until they cried when his mom walked by, trying to look like she wasn't peeking in at them, and almost walked into the doorframe.

"Nothing to see here," she said, sliding back out of view.

"Nothing to see here either," said Karl as Betsy wrapped her arms around his neck and kissed him until he seriously considered giving up on dinner and going straight to dessert.

A wolf whistle came from the living room. It had to have been Nick. "I hear that."

Betsy flushed pink for the millionth time that day, and Karl hoped she'd keep doing that forever.

First thing was first, though, because today marked the first morning that Karl was going to walk back into the shop since Betsy had told her dad the truth about what happened the night he worked late. Was his job still on the line? He'd lied to Frank. Whether or not he would be forgiven remained to be seen.

He stood up tall, took a deep breath, and let it out. He opened the door to the office and stepped inside. Frank wasn't at the desk, but something else was sitting on top of it.

It was a contract.

It was a contract with his name on it.

It was a contract to purchase the shop.

"Yes, yes, yes!" Karl punched the air. He jumped up and down. He picked up his phone, ready to call Betsy, Nick, his parents...everyone. Was he allowed to tell anyone yet? This was incredible. Everything was going to work out. He and Betsy were finally, finally, together. And to top it all off, he would learn everything there was to know about running this place.

He paced back and forth. Where was Frank?

"You done in there?" Frank called from the garage.

"Just about," Karl called back. He punched the air one last time then yelled, "It's safe to come in now."

Chapter Nineteen

In Which Wes is Invited on a Crime Spree

The village of Ephraim waited up ahead with the bay on one side and a hill full of white churches and simple white saltbox houses on the other. What looked beautiful on a normal day took on an ominous aura when Wes considered what he'd found in the bag. It was embarrassing to even have to ask but, Wes reasoned, he wasn't the one who'd brought a bag of... whatever that was on a road trip.

"Oh, that," Patrick said. "I guess I'm going to have to tell you pretty soon anyway." He looked out the window; Wes couldn't see his expression. Just when Wes thought he was going to try to get away with not saying anything more about it, Patrick spoke again. "I'm sorry. I asked you to drive me to my brother's house under false pretences."

"So why are we going?" Wes cut to the chase. What had he gotten himself into? Unless he was about to be told that they were going on some kind of a charity mission-and he couldn't imagine what kind of a charity mission would require the contents of that paper bag-Wes had once again tried and failed in his efforts to be a better man. "I was supposed to be finalizing the details of my wedding today, but I agreed to do this because I thought you wanted to reconcile with your brother." *Wait a minute.* "Do you really have a brother in Ephraim?"

"I do, but he's not here this week. He's out of town."

"Are we going to his house?"

Patrick nodded.

"And are we leaving the contents of that bag at his house?"

Patrick nodded again, and Wes started looking for a convenient place to turn around.

Patrick held out his hands, as if imploring Wes to hear him out. "Everything else I told you is true, with one important difference."

"What's that?" Wes asked blandly, annoyed at having been lied to. What a piece of work this guy was. He'd been cruel to his brother all their lives, and he was still at it. Why couldn't he leave the poor guy alone? And what was Wes going to tell Bea when he got back? *Sorry I couldn't be there to work on our wedding plans. I ended up pranking an old man instead.*

"I'm the nerdy brother," Patrick said, so quietly Wes could barely hear him over the whoosh of the wind rushing past the bus.

"You?"

"Yes." Patrick's eyes flashed. "Leroy was the popular, athletic one. He teased me mercilessly, with my parents egging him on. Like you, I didn't fit in around here as a kid. I didn't even fit in with my own family, and they let me know it. It became like a game for them. When I met my wife in high school, I was so shy I could hardly look at her. She didn't give up on me, though. Later, she told me she'd had her eye on me for a year before we even spoke. She was like me, bookish and sensitive. We were a perfect match. She wouldn't be happy if she could see what I was up to today, but maybe you'll understand when I explain."

"Go ahead." Wes was softening but still skeptical. He hadn't turned the bus around yet, and they'd just arrived at the intersection of Patrick's brother's road and the highway. Wes parked the bus and waited to hear the rest of the story. If it wasn't exceptionally convincing, he could drive right past their destination and no one would ever know they'd been there.

"When my parents died, they left Leroy everything. Well, almost everything. They left me the green couch."

"The one you'd argue about?"

"You got it. I insisted it was green, and when they died, they left me nothing but 'Patrick's favorite *blue* couch'."

Wow. Taunting your son from the grave was really low. Wes didn't like these people. He was starting to understand why Patrick was here. "What are you planning to do?"

"My brother took everything, as the will instructed, but he also took the couch. *Good riddance*, I said. I didn't want anything to do with it."

"So what changed?"

"My wife died. I was all alone, and I got a hankering to destroy that couch once and for all. I knew you had this bus plus the experience of being an underdog, and I thought, once we got here, you might understand."

"Couldn't you have told me what was going on from the start?"

A woman walking by with a little caramel-colored shih tzu looked in at the two men arguing in the bookmobile. If they'd planned on being inconspicuous, there was no chance of that now. Wes gave her a timid wave.

"What would you have said if I asked you to take me on a trip to steal a couch from an 82 year old man?" Patrick asked him.

Wes thought for a moment. It was kind of a no-brainer. "I would've said no."

"What do you say now?"

"I'm going to say yes, but I have to draw the line at whatever you were planning to do with that...is it dog poop?"

"It is. I grabbed it out of Chloe's yard last night."

"What were you going to do with it?"

"I thought about leaving it in place of the couch, in case there was any doubt in Leroy's mind that it was me."

"Dare I ask why you chose that as your calling card?"

"Leroy used to sneak dog poop into my backpack on the way to and from school. He won't have forgotten."

Wes understood the impulse, but he had his limits. "Yes to the couch, no to the dog poop. Deal?"

Patrick beamed. "Deal." They shook on it.

When they arrived at the house, however, a couple of other problems sprang to Wes's mind. Namely, how were they going to get into the house? Once inside, how were they going to carry out the couch? Wes could handle it, and Patrick looked strong enough, but he was eighty years old.

Patrick had an answer for both of those difficulties. "Leroy's neighbor has a key. He's going to let us in and help us lift the couch."

"Nice that he can help, but he doesn't seem like the greatest neighbor. He's letting us in to steal a couch?" Wes followed Patrick to their accomplice's front door.

"He's a great guy, but my brother harasses him all the time. Leroy screams at his kids for 'getting crumbs on the grass' and complains that the guy's leaves are blowing into his yard. Leroy blows them all back. He's earned his enemies fair and square."

When they got to the neighbor's door, a thin man with a gaggle of children running around behind him answered. His eyes darted around the street as he joined them outside. "I've been waiting with the key all morning."

He looked incredibly uncomfortable, and Wes could read the poor guy's mind, because he felt exactly as squeamish as the neighbor looked. He was wondering if this was illegal (almost certainly), whether anyone had seen the bookmobile pull into the driveway (undoubtedly), and how much time he had before the neighbor on the other side, who was outside weeding her perennial border, came over to see what was going on (Wes gave her ten minutes, tops).

"Let's go." Patrick led them up his brother's flagstone steps, and the neighbor let them in.

Unlike its owner, the house was beautiful on the inside. It had high ceilings, rich wood floors, a sparkling chandelier above a long oak table, and expansive windows overlooking the bay. All of the furniture: the chairs that sat side by side near the window, the armchair next to an antique side table, and the couch that faced an elaborate stone fireplace, was crisp white with red and blue throw pillows. A small tattered couch, like a hobo in a dining car full of first class passengers, slouched in a hidden corner of the room. That had to be it. Wes thought it looked more teal than anything else, but he wasn't about to weigh in.

Patrick darted for the couch and gave it a kick. "There it is. The awful thing."

"Do you mind if we hurry?" the neighbor asked. Not waiting for an answer, he picked up one side of the couch and shot a glance at the front door. Wes, sensing the need for urgency as well, picked up the other side, and they hurried to the waiting bookmobile. Wes popped open the back door of the bus, and they were just able to squeeze the couch inside, when they tilted it sideways and angled it just so.

The neighbor, who had already run back to Leroy's house and locked the door, didn't wave goodbye as he darted back to the safety of his own home like a gopher to its hole. With Patrick in the passenger seat and Wes behind the wheel, the bookmobile rolled away from the scene of the crime.

"You did it," Wes said, grinning over at Patrick. "How does it feel?"

Patrick scowled and tapped his finger on his lip. He fiddled with the buttons on his cardigan and swiveled in his seat, looking back at the little-whatever color it was-couch. "I don't know. I don't want to sound ungrateful to you two men, sticking your necks out for me, but I haven't decided how I feel about it yet."

"Maybe it's taking some time to sink in."

"Yeah. Maybe."

They didn't speak as they turned onto the highway and headed for home.

Once again, Wes had a strong suspicion that he knew what the man next to him was thinking. When Wes had returned to Namur as an adult, after vowing he'd never come back, he had a chip on his shoulder. Bea had broken up with him, people in the village thought he was unstable at best, and he wanted nothing more than to prove them all wrong, save the library, and get out of there.

As it turned out, most of the people in the village were kinder than he'd remembered, once he'd given them a chance. Bea, too, had broken up with him on her father's orders, but had gotten brave enough over the years to develop a strong-willed personality and a mind of her own. Her parents had come to love Wes.

This was different, though.

What if Wes had come back and everyone had rejected him all over again? What if they'd never changed their minds about him, had never accepted him? Wes would've left. He wouldn't have saved the library building. (He hadn't been able to do that even though he'd stayed.) Hugh would never have fixed the bookmobile, and Wes wouldn't be driving it home, about to marry Bea.

He would be back in Madison, probably working at the university again, maybe still angry at the people of his hometown. It didn't make logical sense. Who cared what some people in one little village thought of him? Having imaginary friends had been fun. Wes knew they weren't real, but he'd enjoyed his time with them. They were part of who he was, of who he'd become.

It wasn't about logic though, it was about a little voice that sneaked up every now and then, in a moment of uncertainty, and asked, *What if they were right? What if they saw straight through me? Saw something I couldn't see myself. Saw how strange and insignificant I was.*

So how much worse was it for Patrick? How did a person live with knowing that his family, the people who should've loved and accepted him more than anyone else, had rejected him? They'd been wrong to do it. Anyone could see that. Patrick was a grown man who'd lived a long life, one he could look back on and feel proud.

Wes didn't have the answers for how to accept

the past, but one thing was certain: they didn't lie in a tattered old couch. "Your wife sounds like a lovely woman."

Patrick looked out the window with an unfocused gaze and, although his eyes didn't regain their sparkle, a slight smile appeared on his lips. "Oh, she was. She was smart as a whip, and funny too. Most people didn't know that about her, but she would say the funniest things when we were alone together. You would've liked her. She loved to read. She wanted to visit the bookmobile, but she was already sick when you got it up and running. We would've been married sixty years this August. I miss her every day."

"I'm sorry I didn't get to know her better." Wes could remember Patrick's wife, very vaguely, from his childhood. What stood out to Wes was her long hair. It was already silvery gray back then, and beautiful. She had seemed quiet, just as Patrick had said, but in a comfortable, peaceful sort of way.

She'd loved Patrick for who he was, and he'd loved her back.

What else mattered?

"What are you doing next Saturday?" Wes asked. "I'm getting married, and I'd love it if you'd attend."

"Really?" Patrick asked, the sparkle returning to his eyes. "I'd be honored, but don't you need to ask the missus first?"

"No," said Wes. "She'd insist. I know she would."

Chapter Twenty

In Which Two Bloodsuckers Turn Up in Quick Succession

"You can't sit there looking like that and not tell me what happened yesterday." Chloe hadn't been able to focus all morning. Her notepad was covered with doodles of vampires and flowers. It was an interesting insight into her mind.

Betsy knew she wanted to hear every detail of her date with Karl, but Chloe was notorious for dragging out the suspense when she had a secret of her own. It wouldn't kill her to get a dose of her own medicine for a change.

"I'm serious," Chloe continued, flopping her head onto the table. "I can't stand it. Look at you. I wouldn't be surprised if you rose off your chair and started floating around the room."

"I'm happy with how it went," Betsy said, smiling her most enigmatic smile.

"Yes. I can see that. More information, please? This was the event of the year. You don't even know how much everyone was talking about you and Karl at Martel's last night."

No, but Betsy could imagine. People used to tease her about all the time she and Karl spent together. The whole village had assumed something was going on between the two of them, and now that it was, Betsy couldn't believe that it hadn't happened ages ago.

"Alright, I'll tell you a little bit, but...."

There was a knock at the door. Marshmallow sprang into action, leaping up and barking out the window. Chloe groaned dramatically and stomped over to see who was interrupting the beginning of the story of the year.

"We're not buying any..." Chloe stopped speaking; a sharp gasp escaped from her lips. Betsy pushed herself out of the chair to see who had elicited such an un-Chloe like sound.

A middle-aged man with deep black hair, ivory skin, and shamrock green eyes had materialized on the front stoop. He was tall and angular and elegant in slim gray pants and a soft blue t-shirt. Chloe stood there, mouth agape, not saying a thing as Marshmallow tried to edge past her to greet the newcomer with some front paws to the chest and a hearty lick. Betsy, thinking it might be fun to see how long it would take for Chloe to come to, was reassured by the fact that the newcomer looked just as amused as she was.

"Can I come in?" he asked. Was that a Transylvanian accent?

Chloe gasped a second time and the man burst out laughing.

"I'm Noah, your new neighbor," he said, extending his hand and dropping the accent. It was replaced by a slight southern drawl.

"Are you though?" Chloe asked, taking it gingerly, as though he'd just offered her a slimy trout to grip.

"I'm not a vampire. Are you worried that I'm a vampire?" How did he know?

Chloe scoffed. "No..." She narrowed her eyes. "Prove it."

He sighed and pulled a mirror out of his back pocket. He held it up behind his head and, sure enough, his dark hair reflected back at them. "This happens to me more often than you'd expect. Do you want to take a look at the mirror to make sure it's real?"

"Sure." Chloe acted all casual about it, but Betsy had no doubt that would've been her next question if he hadn't offered. She looked at herself in the mirror. "Do I really look like that right now? Yikes. Anyway, you check out. Come on in. We work from home, so the kitchen table's kind of messy, but I'll make a space for you. Do you want some coffee?"

"I'd love some," he said, "but I can't stay long. The daylight drains me of my vital energy."

Chloe spun around to face him.

"I'm kidding. Clearly, we need to talk." Noah followed her into the kitchen, with Marshmallow and Betsy trailing behind. She couldn't believe Chloe was inviting him in. Not because Betsy really thought he was a vampire, but because her older sister clearly hadn't made up her mind yet one way or the other.

Betsy introduced herself to Noah, and he shook her hand as well. His hand was shockingly cold to the touch. Chloe wouldn't have missed that either.

"Sorry about the other day," Noah said as he sat down at the table. Chloe shuffled her papers out of the way in front of him. "I appreciated the muffins, but I was trying to stay in character. It's why I keep to myself."

Chloe nodded in understanding. Were these two going to go on as if they both understood exactly what the other was thinking? He knew she thought he was a vampire, and she understood why he needed to act like one...Betsy didn't understand a word of it.

"I thought it might've been that. That, or you really were one of the undead. I'm not one hundred percent convinced you're not, but we'll iron that out eventually." Chloe handed him a mug of coffee and watched as he took a sip.

"This doesn't prove anything, you know," he said. "Orpheus Adair is able to eat and drink, but it doesn't do anything to sustain him."

Chloe concurred. "And he can go outside during the day, but only briefly."

"Exactly."

"But the mirror thing..."

"Maybe I've overcome it."

Chloe sat down across from him and gulped down the rest of her cold coffee. "That's a good point."

Betsy had finally had enough. "Guys, I don't mean to be dense, but I don't understand what's going on." She didn't like to be a busybody, but *come on*, this was going too far.

"Noah writes the Nina Striker books," Chloe

explained.

"You do?" Betsy asked, looking to him for confirmation.

He nodded. "How did you figure it out?"

"I accidentally got a letter addressed to Orpheus Adair in my mailbox," Chloe explained. "I looked up the author of the books, and he looks just like you. I figured you were using a pen name."

"I am. I like my privacy. I'm actually surprised you could find a picture of me. I try to keep those under wraps."

"I'm a determined woman." That was an understatement if ever Betsy had heard one. "Is all your mail addressed to Orpheus?"

"No, you must've gotten a letter from my agent. He thinks he's being funny. Anyway, now that you know who I am, I have a request." For the first time since he'd arrived, Noah looked uncomfortable. If being accused of being a vampire couldn't do that, it should be interesting to see what could. "First, please don't tell anyone that I'm here. I've been working on the final Nina book for years, and a select group of fans have gone from impatient to frighteningly irate."

"My lips are sealed." Chloe zipped them up with the end of her pen.

"Second, I knew you figured out there was something going on with me, because you look at my house all the time. It's distracting. Could you stop doing that?"

"Sure," said Chloe. Would she really, though?

"The reason you never see me is because, when I'm writing my books, I like to stay in character. It helps me get into the heads of the people I'm writing about. I stay awake at night and pretend I live in a run-down old lumber baron's house in the middle of an isolated wood."

"Like Orpheus."

"Right. Also, I don't care for other people very much, and it's a convenient excuse. No offense."

"None taken. Can I make a request too?"

Betsy gave her a warning look, which Chloe ignored.

"Go ahead," said Noah.

"If you ever do see me outside, can you give me an enigmatic smoldering glower, like you're bent on world domination, and I'll stop at nothing to prevent that from happening, but we're undeniably bound to each other with a love that will last eternally?"

If Noah had been embarrassed about his request, Chloe should've been doubly so, but no one in the room except Betsy seemed to think there was anything even remotely unusual about it. Noah nodded as simply as if she'd just asked him if he'd like a piece of pie. "You're Nina then?"

"I am."

"Yeah. I like it, but you don't actually live next to me. This is a hovel you've constructed in the woods near the outskirts of my property for the purposes of surveillance. You don't think I know it's there, but I do."

"I love it. Where does that leave Betsy?"

"I'm fine," said Betsy, who didn't feel the need to be involved with...whatever this was.

"No. You have to be part of it," Chloe insisted. "You're in and out of my hovel almost every day."

Betsy sighed. "How about I'm your pregnant sister, and you have to keep me safe, because a red haired mechanic vampire has fallen in love with me." Oh well, it was all in fun. Chloe and Noah adored the idea.

They visited for at least another hour. It turned out that Noah's dislike of people didn't extend to those who wanted to live out his books in real life. He was actually a pretty interesting guy, and Betsy considered reading the Nina books herself, partly because she knew the author, and partly because it would render Chloe more predictable and therefore slightly less dangerous.

When Noah left, Chloe gushed for a while, but it didn't take long for her to come back to the subject of Betsy and Karl. Before Betsy could begin the story of their first date, however, a knock at the door interrupted her once again.

What now?

It was George.

And by the end of his visit, he made Betsy wish there'd been an actual vampire on Chloe's front stoop, rather than the no-good, scheming creep who stood there instead.

Betsy had answered the door this time, and George strode inside with a "We need to talk."

"Hi," Betsy said, annoyed. What was he doing

here? She was working. Why didn't he ever give her any warning?

He slipped his glasses onto the top of his head and gave her a serious, concerned stare. "Can we talk somewhere private?"

Chloe had come halfway into the room. She stood in the doorway with a scowl on her face. "What's up?" she asked.

George turned to her slowly, as if she was testing his patience. "There's something I need to discuss, with *Betsy*." His tone made it clear that he was telling her to leave. Chloe's stance made it clear there was no way she was budging.

"We can talk here," Betsy said. "I tell Chloe everything anyway. We don't have any secrets." What could George possibly have to say to her that required him to race all the way here and talk to her in person? He was acting very strange. Usually so cool and relaxed, George was fidgety, his jaw as tense as if it had been frozen in place.

"Fine, but I'm not sure you're going to want her to hear this."

"What do you mean? You're scaring me. Just tell me what's going on."

"It's about Karl. Is it true that you're seeing him?"

"Yes...is that what this is about? Because you and I are not together. You broke up with me months ago."

Chloe leaned against the door frame, folding her arms across her chest. Little did George know, he was also dealing with Nina. Betsy shot a pleading look at her sister, hoping she wouldn't lose it in the face of George's nonsense.

"I know," said George, "and maybe that was a mistake. I don't know, but one thing is certain: we're having a baby together. I need to look out for you. I should have a say in the kind of people you're spending time with, the kind of people who will be in my daughter's life."

"Maybe you could start by worrying about how little *you've* been involved in your daughter's life," said Chloe. George glared at her and she glared back.

"Can we go somewhere else?" he asked again.

"I'd prefer to stay right here, thank you." Betsy felt herself losing her patience already, and she was well aware that George hadn't said all he'd come here to say.

George stood taller, his arrogant smirk returning in full force. "You know what? That's perfect. You should both hear this, so you understand who you've gotten yourself involved with."

"Karl and I have been friends for years. I have no illusions about what kind of a person he is. I'm lucky to have him in my life." She put her hand on her belly. "In her life, too."

"In that case, I'm sorry to have to shatter your image of him." His grin widened. He wasn't sorry at all. "He's a thief. The summer after his senior year, I caught him taking money from Tom's farm stand."

"You're lying. Karl would never do that."

Would he? It had been a difficult year. Both boys' shoes had had holes in the toes, and Nick's pants had gotten much too short before Betsy finally bought him a pair or two that fit.

George ignored her protestations. "I just happened to be there. I was visiting for the weekend over the summer and stopped by the stand to grab some of Tom's tomatoes for my mom. I saw Karl pull the money out with my own eyes. I confronted him, told him if I saw him doing it again, I'd tell Tom. He admitted that he'd done it and begged me not tell. He even offered to split the money with me. I didn't take it, of course. I also didn't end up telling anyone, but I doubt it was the first time he'd been stealing. I also doubt it was the last."

Maybe it was true. Maybe Karl had stolen from Tom when he was eighteen, but he wasn't a thief. He was one of the good guys. Betsy knew it. She knew it like she knew that the man standing before her wasn't. He'd proven it to her in so many ways, and he'd confirmed it today.

"It's possible you're telling the truth, but that was a long time ago. Karl's not like that. His family was having financial difficulties. You know what happened to his dad."

George was unmoved. "That may be, but there's no excuse for stealing. We're a tight community. We have to be able to trust each other. I know your father will agree with me."

"My father? What are you talking about?"

"I'd hoped you'd see reason, but if you won't,

and you continue to spend time with someone who has a sketchy past, I'll have no choice but to tell your dad what kind of a man he has working for him, what kind of a man is dating his youngest daughter."

George couldn't do this. Karl had almost lost his job because of Betsy, and here it was, happening all over again.

"Get out." While Betsy agonized, Chloe had crossed the room and inserted herself between her and George.

"Excuse me?" George's voice dripped with disdain.

"You heard me. Get. Out. Of. My. House."

George snapped his sunglasses down and headed for the door. "That's fine. I'm gone. I don't need this. I'm going to do what I have to do to protect my child." He turned to Betsy, who had wrapped her arms around herself, trying to slow the shaking that had spread from her knees to the rest of her body. "If I don't hear from you this week, with a promise not to see Karl again, I will be getting in touch with your dad on Friday."

He left the house and drove away.

Chapter Twenty-One

In Which Two Hearts are Broken

"It's true." Karl stood, leaving Betsy on his couch with her hands clasped together, tears streaking her face. "I stole from Tom, and one of the times-the third or fourth maybe-George caught me. I couldn't deny it. He'd seen me take the money," Karl continued. "Before I'd gone over there that day, I'd vowed it was going to be my last time, but George said, if I didn't keep taking the money and splitting it with him, he'd tell everyone. Thinking back, I can't believe I agreed to it, but I was young and I couldn't do that to my parents. If they'd known I was stealing to buy food and clothes and stuff...They were barely holding on as it was." He looked out his bay window with his back to Betsy, his fist clenched so tightly his nails pressed into his calloused palms.

"It went on for the rest of the summer. I can't believe Tom never figured it out, but somehow he didn't. I made sure not to take too much, but it was a miracle I wasn't caught. At the end of the year, when I sent George his final payment, I included a letter that said I was done, that I couldn't be blackmailed anymore. I never stole anything again, and I never heard from George again either, not about that."

"I'm so sorry. This is all my fault," Betsy squeaked out from behind him.

He turned around and strode over to the couch, sitting down next to her and gathering her face up in his hands. "This is not your fault. I made a bad choice. It's no one else's fault but mine. I could blame George, but I'm the one who started this."

Betsy shook her head. "George is only digging it back up because you got involved with me. He never would've mentioned it again otherwise." Karl's heart was breaking to have hurt her. Betsy couldn't even look at him. "I can't see you anymore," she said, new resolve creeping into her voice as she struggled to keep it steady. "It's not because of the money. I believe you when you say you've never done it again, but I'm not going to be the reason you lose your job, your reputation."

He'd lose more than that. He hadn't told her about buying the shop yet. Nothing was set in stone. Once her dad learned about Karl's past, the deal was sure to be off. Doing extra work on the side was one thing, stealing from an old farmer was quite another.

"I won't accept that." Karl slid closer to her, leaning in so she couldn't avoid looking him in the eye. "I won't let George dictate what happens between us. That's between you and me."

Betsy looked back at him as if begging him to understand why she was doing this. "I'm not willing to let you throw away your life for me. It was selfish of me to let my silly feelings run away with me in the first place. It's the story of my life, and you deserve better."

How could Karl convince her that this wasn't her fault, that she was the bright spot in every moment of darkness in his life? "Is that what you really think? That you're selfish and silly? Because nothing could be further from the truth. I don't know how to show you what I see when I look at you, but I'm not giving up until I figure it out."

"I'm not giving you a choice. You know what will happen if people in this town find out you stole from Tom. It won't just be my dad. No one will hire you. For all his nonsense, George has influence over people somehow. People don't know what he's really like. If he goes to my dad on Friday, you'll have to move if you want to find a job. What then? What will happen to your parents? What will happen to Nick?"

She was right, but is this how Karl wanted to live his life? Afraid of being found out? Blackmailed by the likes of George? "He may have been able to scare me back then, but I'm not playing his games any more. If you don't want to be with me..."

"I do. You know I do, but I won't be the reason you can't take care of the people you love."

"I love *you*. Don't you get it? I'm crazy about you. There's no way I'm going to let anyone blackmail me into letting you go."

Betsy covered her face with her hands, her shoulders shaking. "I'm so sorry. I'm so sorry, Karl." She heaved herself off of the couch.

"Please don't go. Let's talk about this."

She stumbled out the door. "I'm sorry. I can't. It's too much."

Should Karl follow her? Letting Betsy go caused a moment of pain so acute he'd had to shut the door and lean his whole body against it to keep from going after her, from calling her back. It took everything he had within him not to fling open the door and jump in front of her car to stop her from leaving, but he knew her too well. If she thought she could save him by staying away, then that's what she would do. It was up to Karl to fix this. He knew what he had to do, and he'd waste no time in getting it done.

If George thought Karl would take this lying down, he'd made a major miscalculation. He hadn't accounted for the fact that Karl had seen what it meant to fight. This nonsense? It was nothing, nothing at all.

***

Tom and his wife Florence sat on the front porch of their old Belgian farmhouse in identical rocking chairs, talking and laughing together. They waved as Karl got out of his truck and headed towards them. Stepping hesitantly at first, struck anew by the possible consequences of what he was about to do, Karl picked up speed as he got closer. He had practiced what he was going to say on the way over, but now that he was here the words were jumbling around in his mind like damp clothes in a dryer. He took a deep breath, steadied himself, and climbed the porch steps.

"Hello, Karl. It's a lovely evening. Did you come to join us for some iced tea?" Florence asked, motioning to a third chair. Karl was tempted to say yes, he was here for nothing more than a quiet visit. He would sit on the porch with Tom and Florence and look out on the fields, sipping tea with a wedge of lemon and listening to Tom's report on the village news he'd gathered from his favorite red bench.

If only.

"No thank you. I came to talk to the two of you. I'm sorry to interrupt you with something like this, but there's something I'd like to confess."

Florence looked perplexed, but Tom nodded his head in understanding, stood up from his rocker, and joined Karl by the stairs.

"We're going to take a little walk," Tom told his wife. "Don't go inside, though. I need to finish my story about the Ed and the rooster. You're going to want to hear that one, too." He elbowed Karl and chuckled. "Come along, I'll show you the new setup in my coop."

Why was Tom acting like he knew why Karl was here? *Did* he know? Had George gotten to him already?

When they were out of earshot, Tom answered Karl's unspoken questions. "I know why you're here, and I'm going to spare you the discomfort of having to tell me. If I had to do it over again, I'd have done it differently, but I'm guessing you're feeling the same way, so we won't be too hard on each other. Deal?"

"You know why I'm here?"

"Unless there's something else I don't know about, and somehow I doubt there's much I'm not aware of around here, you're here to confess to swiping money from my farm stand back in the day."

"How did you find out?"

"I saw you do it. I thought about saying something, but I didn't want to embarrass you. I knew what was going on over at your house and thought of it as helping out."

"And the other times?"

"I was putting money in there myself. Did you really think my farm stand was that profitable?" He laughed. "I only wish."

They'd reached the chicken coop by now, a wooden shed painted green with tan trim. The chickens and rooster milled about outside, a mix of black and buff brown ones, raking the grass with their talons, their heads jerking and bobbing as they snatched at bugs and scraps of food.

"I'm so sorry," said Karl. There was a small part of him that was relieved that Tom knew and didn't mind, but what difference did it make, really? Karl hadn't known that when he'd done it.

"No, I'm sorry," said Tom. "I should've told you I'd seen you and offered to help. That's what I would've done today. Maybe I thought it would've embarrassed you. I can't honestly remember, but it ended with you feeling like a thief."

"Well, I was," Karl pointed out.

"What were you doing with that money? Buying cigarettes and beer probably." Tom winked at him. "I knew what you were up to. I didn't have as much time on my hands back then as I do now, but I had an eye for what was going on. It's not purely out of insufferable nosiness that I pay attention to the happenings around here. Don't ask my wife to weigh in on that, though."

"I'd like to pay you back," said Karl, but Tom wouldn't hear of it.

"Don't talk nonsense. It was nothing."

"It wasn't nothing to me. I'd like to do something to repay you. Is there anything you need help with around here?"

"You know what? There is something. Pay it forward to someone else. Keep your eyes open, and if you see someone who needs help some time, step up and help them. I suspect you'd reach out anyway, but give a thought to me when you do."

"Done." Karl said, and he and Tom shook on it.

"I have one more question for you," Tom said.

"Sure."

"Why now?"

"Why am I telling you now?"

"Right. I appreciate your honesty, but I thought of it as water under the bridge."

"If I tell you, will you please keep it between us?"

"Of course." Tom picked up a handful of sticks from amongst the grass and tossed them along the side of the chicken coop, startling a gaggle of hens.

"Someone else knew that I was taking the money. They've threatened to tell my boss. I decided it might be better coming from me than him. Besides, it felt like the right thing to do."

"I hate to make assumptions, but I'm going to ask anyway. Is it George?"

Karl turned to Tom in surprise. "How did you know?"

"Because of nosiness." He barked out a laugh. "Word around town was that you and Betsy were stepping out together last weekend. I bet George took an interest in that news as well."

Karl nodded.

"Let's just say I've taken the measure of George," said Tom. "He and I are going to have a little talk. I know more about George and his dealings than either he or I would like. I'm not going to expose what I know about him, but I guarantee he'll think twice before he bothers you again."

Karl couldn't say he was sorry to hear that. "Thank you Tom, but do you think I should come clean to Frank anyway?"

"Naw. This was between you and me. It was a long time ago. We'd do things differently if we had the chance. Let's leave it at that. Now come on over and visit." Tom walked back across the grass, headed for the comfort of his shady porch. A grateful Karl followed behind him.

Chapter Twenty-Two

In Which the Goats Get the Upper Hand

There were at least ten goats in the garden along the split rail fence, chomping fiercely on shocks of fluffy lettuce and the squash vines that Bea had just transferred into the garden from the greenhouse.

This wasn't good. Bea had worked all day yesterday transplanting seedlings, and at least half of them had been mowed to the ground. They were even going after her raspberries, her delicious, beautiful raspberries that would produce jewel bright red and yellow berries in a matter of months, if they weren't all demolished by these eating machines. Goatzart and Billy Nye the Goat Guy yanked on the brambles and chomped chunks off of them as if they were smooth whips of licorice rather than spike covered menaces.

Wes looked around the yard. Where was everyone? They must be inside, getting ready for lunch. Should Wes run inside and get them? It had been a rough couple of weeks, and this fiasco would do nothing towards making Bea feel better.

No. Let them stay inside, blissfully unaware of the chaos unfolding out here.

Maybe Wes could tackle these guys on his own.

He'd usher them back into their enclosure, find the weak spot that had allowed them to escape, then head in for lunch without anyone being the wiser. Bea was sure to notice the destruction in her garden, but if Wes did some quick cleaning up, she might chalk it up to rabbits.

How to get them all to move though?

Wes surveyed the crowd. He'd start with Vincent, who was eyeing up some rhubarb leaves. She hated him. The other goats would seem easy in comparison. Wes approached her slowly, speaking in a soothing voice and taking slow, easy steps.

"Hey, Vinnie. We're going to head back into the comfy barn. I'll just ease you over..." He nudged her with his palm and she, amazingly, took a couple of steps in the direction he wanted her to go. This could be easier than he'd thought. He gave her another nudge, and another, and pretty soon she was back in the barn.

Wes brushed his hands together. Success.

He approached Spotty next and followed the exact same procedure. She walked placidly into the barn. Two down, thirteen to go. Who next?

Wait.

Was that Vincent van Goat chomping on the butter lettuce? White body? Check. Brown spots? Check. An evil eye directed at Wes as she swallowed a gigantic mouthful of lettuce? Yup. It was the very same goat who'd just walked back so complacently moments ago. Why wasn't she in the barn where he'd left her? There must be a spot in the fence where they were getting through.

Wes headed towards the barn, getting ready to walk around the fence line, when he spied Spotty, wiggling through a hole in the far side. He sprinted towards her. "Oh no you don't." Feet flying, he made his way across the uneven ground. About halfway there, he tripped in a divot in the grass, flying face first. Grass stains covered his palms and the front of his shorts.

Wes looked up with beady, determined eyes that he hoped looked at least a little bit like Ed's. He wouldn't let these goats get the better of him.

Wes sprang back up and raced to the hole just as Spotty broke free. She capered past him, weaving her way back to the raspberry patch. Those rascals. They were happily being ushered back because they knew they had an escape route.

Wes would fix that in short order. He strode over to the spot where Spotty had busted loose. A piece of the fence had broken off, probably from the goats leaning on it, and had left a hole just big enough for them to wiggle their way through. Wes pulled the piece over and wrapped it around an adjacent tine, blocking the hole. It was a temporary fix, but it should hold while he shunted these rascals into the barn.

He jogged back to the garden, a little more carefully this time, and confronted Vincent. "No more mister nice guy. You're going into the barn, and you're going to stay there. You don't belong out here. And after everything Bea does for you." He shook his head.

Vincent didn't even have the decency to look

ashamed.

Vincent and Spotty went back into the barn as easily as before, and Wes watched with satisfaction as they trotted over to the weak spot in the fence and tried to get out, to no avail. He'd outsmarted him. Wesley Jacquemart was at least as intelligent as a bunch of goats.

Who next? The Great Goatsby should be pretty easy to cajole. He nudged her along and, sure enough, she was putty in Wes's hands. This should be...

You've got to be kidding me.

Spotty and Vincent were back in the garden. Wes ran to the hole in the fence. It was bigger than ever. "I give up," he yelled. "You win! Happy? You've defeated me, but just you wait. I'm going to get a bigger, better fence, and you'll never...Oh. Hi Bea."

Bea, who had maybe, possibly, been alerted to Wes's presence when he started yelling at the goats at the top of his lungs, laughed so hard she was bent double, holding her sides. "I take it there's a hole over there?" she called between gasps.

"Um...yes. Yes, there is." Wes tried to pull himself together, but he was well aware of how his hair stuck straight up from his head, and the way his clothes were covered in dirt and grass.

"Stay there and guard the hole while I get them back into the barn." Wes watched in amazement as Bea led them in three at a time. How did she do it? They looked up at her with innocent expressions on their faces, as if they hadn't just been tormenting her fiancé until he was reduced to a hysterical shouting mess.

The goats casually strolled up to The Hole, as Wes had not so affectionately named it, and acted as if they'd just happened to be stopping by and had no interest in whether or not it was still available as an awesome escape route. Wes gave them a haughty glare. There was no doubt in his mind they'd win him over again with their funny antics and their affectionate nuzzles, but now was not that time.

Joining him at The Hole, Bea brushed down the front of his shirt and picked a piece of straw out of his hair. "Do I need to ask what happened?"

"Nope. It's exactly what it looks like."

"I thought so. I'm going to get something to patch up this fence. Do you mind waiting here?"

"Not at all." Wes scratched Spotty's forehead. He was softening already.

Bea came back with a section of fence. "I should replace a lot of this. It's getting worn out. These guys are hard on fences."

"Sorry about your garden," said Wes as he helped Bea tie the panel into place. "I must've caught them pretty early in their feeding frenzy, because it doesn't look too terrible."

"No. I think you caught them just in time. Another five minutes and I'd have been left with a dirt patch formerly known as my garden. From the looks of it, you put up a heroic fight."

"I did. I really did. Me versus the goats. I think we may have to declare the goats the winners on this one."

"But you ultimately thwarted them. We'll call it a tie." Bea gave a brief glance towards her raspberry patch and winced a little. "It's not so bad. It looks like we'll still have raspberries this year, so that's a positive. Now that they've had a taste of the garden, they're going to be trying extra hard to break loose. We'll have to be on our guard." Bea took his hand and they headed back to the house. Halfway there she stopped, turning to face him. "You know what I just realized? After this week, you'll be living here too. It'll be so different. In a wonderful way." She added.

"Reporting in for goat guard duty." He saluted her.

"Yes. They'll be shocked. Isn't it exciting though? I can't wait to wake up every morning together and fall asleep next to you at night. It doesn't seem real."

Wes looked at Bea, her sweet face tilted up to his. What could he say? There was no way to adequately express to her what her love had done for him. As far as he could tell, he'd done nothing to deserve it. It had all come down to pure luck. "I can't wait either, and I'm sorry I didn't come with you to finalize the plans yesterday. I should've been there." He pulled her close to him and Bea nestled her head into his chest.

"Thanks," she said, her voice vibrating against his chest. "I know it meant a lot to you to help Patrick reunite with his brother, but it would've been nice if you'd joined me."

Should he tell her the real reason he and Patrick

went to Ephraim? Nah. He'd save it for another day. It was a long story, and he'd rather talk about their future right now. "How did everything look over at the barn?"

"Perfect. It's going to be amazing." She paused, looking thoughtful. "I know this is all a lot for you to take on, and I want you to know how much I believe in you and in us. I'm so grateful to have you by my side. I've never met anyone like you, and I can't believe I get to be the one to marry you."

And here Wes was thinking he was the lucky one. Maybe that was the secret to marital success: each person thinking they'd gotten the better deal. He'd tried to keep his worries from her, but he should've known Bea would be onto him. "I was doing a lot of thinking yesterday," he said.

"What about?"

"About what a big deal it is when you find someone who loves you for who you really are."

"You're easy to love, Wes. I wouldn't change you if I could."

"Likewise," he said. They went inside for lunch.

Wes said hello to Harvey and Claudette then went into the bathroom to clean up. He washed his face, picked a couple more pieces of grass and straw from his hair, and scrubbed his palms. As he was turning around to go, a little green M&M magnet in the corner of the room caught his eye. Bending down and picking it up, Wes slipped it into his pocket.

Now where to hide it?

Chapter Twenty-Three

In Which Evidence is Presented

Betsy had scolded herself into getting out of bed this morning. She'd thrown on some clothes, dragged herself down the stairs, tried to eat breakfast, and slumped over to Chloe's house before her mutinous body, which felt brick heavy, could convince her brain to call in sick and barricade herself in her bedroom.

Karl had come to her house yesterday evening. He'd told her what had happened when he went to Tom's house, how certain he was that George wouldn't be a problem anymore. He looked so hopeful and triumphant. There was no longer a barrier between the two of them. They could be together, happily skipping off into the sunset without a worry in the world.

Except they couldn't.

Because Betsy would have to be delusional to think that this would be the last time she'd cause problems for Karl. He'd been going along just fine for over a year before they'd gotten involved. Things had been looking up. Then he'd gotten involved with her, and *bam,* his boss was on the cusp of firing him and he was about to be exposed as a thief before the entire village.

Betsy had made a huge mistake in letting him into her vortex of nonsense, but it wasn't too late to make sure he stayed out, starting now. When she told him so, Karl hadn't tried to convince her to change her mind. He'd gotten quiet instead, and his look of determination said everything that he hadn't. He wasn't giving up.

That shift-from elation to steely determination-would have been almost imperceptible to anyone who hadn't known him for ages. But Betsy had picked up on it immediately; it had nearly made her change her mind.

How could she let him go? This man who would do anything for her, who would take on any challenge so they could be together?

What made it so difficult was the exact same thing that made it so necessary.

Because he *would* do anything for her, and she wasn't going to let him sacrifice even a sliver of his happiness due to her carelessness.

Chloe hadn't said anything about their breakup when Betsy came in this morning. Betsy had asked her not to. They'd talked on the phone last night after Karl left. Chloe had offered to come over, but Betsy wanted to be alone.

She'd sobbed then, as Chloe listened in silence on the other end. Betsy was full of sadness for herself, but more than that, she cried for Karl and the pain she knew she was causing him. She only hoped that, in his case, anyway, it would be short lived. He'd move on eventually, better off in the long run without her.

Back at Chloe's house, Betsy tried to get her mind back on work. The e-mails were the usual lot: some questions, some forms to fill out, a few invoices...and something from Gadgetgal.

Should she read it? It was probably something sweet that would make her feel even worse. She wasn't going to torture herself. She scrolled on, replying to a couple of e-mails then going back to re-read them, unsure what she'd even written. Thankfully, they looked alright.

Her phone buzzed. It was a message from Karl. *Please read it,* it said. She set her phone on the table upside down and carried on with her work.

She sighed. Today would be the most difficult, but it would get better. She needed to stay strong.

The doorbell rang. Chloe jumped up to answer it.

Betsy ran over to block her way. "Don't. It's probably Karl."

Chloe looked ready to say something in reply, but shook her head instead and walked back to the table. Betsy went to the window and looked outside. There was nobody there. That was odd.

Her phone, still perched on the edge of the table, buzzed again. What now?

It was Karl again. *Open the door. I'm not there. There's something on the porch. It's for Chloe.*

"Fine," she said to her phone. "I'll get it, but only because it's for Chloe."

"Are you talking to me?" Chloe had dived

straight back into her work.

"No. Just arguing with my phone."

Chloe nodded in understanding, and Betsy made her way over to the door. She opened it and looked around. Karl had been telling the truth. There was no one there, but there was a package leaning up against the house next to the door. It was an ordinary cardboard box with Chloe's name written across it in black marker.

It had to have been from Karl, but what could it be?

Picking up the box, Betsy carried it over to the table and set it in front of Chloe.

"For me?" she asked. "I wasn't expecting anything."

"It's from Karl. He sent me a message a minute ago."

"Huh. Is it okay if I open it?"

Betsy was tempted to say no, but it was for Chloe, after all. "I suppose it's fine, but if he's trying to get me to change my mind, don't tell me what it is." Betsy sat down across from Chloe and tried not to watch as she slit open the package and opened the box.

"It's a pile of papers."

"What?" Betsy couldn't resist peeking. Standing up a little, she peered over the edge of the box. Karl's handwriting zigzagged across the top page. She averted her eyes. It had to be a message for her. "What does it say?"

"Are you sure you want to know?"

Betsy nodded, so Chloe read. "It says: *Dear Chloe, A close friend and I are having a disagreement. She remembers things one way, and I remember them another. Memories can be tricky things, so I thought it might be helpful to have an objective third party take a look at some information. Please read this to Betsy, not to change her mind, just to let her see the evidence I've compiled, and let her know what you make of all of this. Thanks for your help, Karl*"

Chloe looked up at Betsy, whose stomach was doing back flips. Evidence? What was he talking about? "Do you want me to go on?" Chloe asked.

As he'd likely anticipated, Betsy's curiosity got the best of her. She nodded, and Chloe flipped the first page to reveal the one below. There was a photo of a group of kids at one of Karl's birthday parties affixed to the top with writing underneath. Betsy joined Chloe on the other side of the table and, side by side, they read.

The first item for your consideration is from my tenth birthday. My dad got a parrot piñata. I was obsessed with pirates and had been asking for one since my last birthday, so it was a huge deal. We were in line taking turns hitting it when the kid in front of me (who was huge for a ten-year-old, by the way) clocked me in the head. I went crashing to the ground. Blood gushed from my head, kids ran around screaming, and my party was over almost as soon as it had begun. All the other kids got picked up by their parents, but Betsy refused to go home until she was sure I would be okay. She held my hand and told me funny stories until my parents decided it was bad enough to rush me to the ER. I needed six stitches. When I got home, I found that Betsy had made a sign and stuck it to my front door.

They flipped the page and there it was: a yellowing crumpled construction paper sign that said *Get Well Soon Karrrrl.* She'd drawn pirate stuff all over it: skulls, treasure chests, palm trees, and little cartoonish pirates with peg legs and eye patches. Betsy remembered making that sign as clearly as if she'd done it yesterday. She'd been so sorry for Karl, having his birthday ruined like that.

Chloe didn't say anything. She glanced at Betsy then pulled out the sign to reveal the next page. On the top of this one was a picture of thirteen-year-old Karl with his arms wrapped around the tummy of little toddler Nick. Nick was standing, but he must have just started walking, because he looked so very tiny.

When Nick was born, I was disgusted with the whole thing. I'd been an only child all my life, and then this little wailing munchkin showed up, taking up my parents' time and keeping me awake. Betsy adored him though, and (as much as I hate to admit it) I followed her lead with pretty much everything, this included. It would've been a hard sell coming from anyone else, but she showed me how much fun it was to have a little brother. She'd read him stories, dress him up, and help him create crazy block towers, and pretty soon I was getting in on the fun too. She invited Nick into our inner circle, and there he stayed. She was right about that. He's a great guy. I like to think I would've figured it out eventually, but you never know.

Chloe flipped to the next page. It was a picture of Karl, in his late teens probably, standing next to his dad, who was now in a wheelchair.

When my dad got hurt, all of our lives changed. Most of my friends had gone off to college, and the ones that hadn't were into going out to the bars or messing around on their snowmobiles or ATVs. I didn't have time for that stuff anymore, and most people kind of forgot about me after a while. It hurt, but I didn't have a right to complain about loneliness or a few lost buddies when my dad had lost so much more. Guess who didn't forget about me, though? Betsy. She called me or came over almost every day without me ever having to ask. She'd hang out with us at home and do boring stuff, like watch the same old movies that we'd watched a hundred times or make puzzles. She probably thought it wasn't a big deal, but it was. It was a really big deal, actually.

"Chloe?" Betsy said, before she could turn another page. "Can we read the rest of these with Karl?"

Betsy didn't want to wait any longer and, thankfully, Chloe didn't hesitate. "Call him. Please."

Betsy grabbed her phone. She dialed.

He answered right away. "Hi…"

"Karl?" she interrupted. "I'm an idiot, okay? I'm so sorry. I love you too." He didn't say anything for a moment, and she held her breath, praying he'd forgive her for pushing him away.

"Yeah. I know you do."

"Oh my gosh. You are unbelievable."

"Thanks. I bet it's one of the things you love about me."

"Let's just say I admire your persistence." *Such a show-off.* She wiped a tear from her cheek. "I wanted you to be happy, and I felt like I was keeping you from that, but…" She didn't know what more to say. He'd proven his point. She wasn't perfect, but she'd been there for him, and he'd been there for her too, even when she'd made mistakes, even when she hadn't seen the obvious standing in front of her in all his red haired, thick bearded, grease smudged glory. "Will you come back over here?" she asked.

He pushed open the door and stepped inside, sliding his phone into his pocket. She kept hers up to her ear, not believing what she was seeing. How had he known she'd ask him to come back?

But of course he did. They'd known each other forever.

"I'll be upstairs," Chloe called from the second-floor landing.

Betsy and Karl stood there smiling at each other, and Betsy didn't feel the need to say a word. She crossed the room in a single breath and flew into his arms, and as he held her, as she pressed her lips to his, as the world around them faded away, she knew she was exactly where she was meant to be with exactly the right person.

Chapter Twenty-Four

In Which Karl Has Another Tense Day

"Can you stay late tonight? Gotta talk to you about something." Frank leaned against the side of Old Blue while Karl changed the tires. Frank was wearing his new green coveralls, the ones that weren't nearly black with grease. The last time Frank had worn them was the day of his anniversary. His wife Tammi had stopped in to bring them pizza for lunch, and Frank had actually smiled. Twice.

"Sure, of course." Karl acted as if this typically vague question didn't concern him in the least, but *come on.* It had been a rough couple of weeks. His nerves needed some time to knit back together before anything more was sprung upon him. A couple of weeks at minimum would've been appreciated.

Frank went back into the office without another word, leaving Karl to wonder what they'd be discussing. Had he found out his mechanic was dating his youngest daughter? It would be a miracle if he hadn't, and it didn't take a lifetime of knowing him to see that Frank was an "I'm just going to clean my gun while we discuss your intentions" kind of a guy.

Karl could handle whatever questions came his

way when it came to Betsy. Now that they were together, there was no way he was going to let her or anyone who cared about her down. Although he'd convinced her of her positive influence on his life, he and Betsy still went through the rest of the box, ending with a picture of them at his parents' kitchen table on their first official date.

Nearly finished with the truck, Karl was securing the last tire when Chloe walked in. "Are you being nice to Old Blue?" she asked, taking a seat at the edge of the room to watch the rest of the proceedings.

Karl swung his hand to his heart, offended that she'd think he would be anything less than meticulously careful. When it came to her truck and her dog, Chloe didn't mess around. "I'm nearly finished," he said. Should he ask her if she knew what was up with her dad? Why not? There was no harm in asking.

She didn't have a clue. "Sorry, but to be honest, it's kind of satisfying to see someone else squirm beneath his gaze. I had to grow up with him."

"Thanks. That does put things in perspective." He tossed Chloe her keys. "Let me finish up here, and you should be good to go."

Chloe crossed her legs and leaned back in the chair, clearly enjoying the warm day and looking forward to getting her truck back.

"Did you see Betsy this morning?" he asked her, trying to keep the silly grin forming on his face from making his voice go wobbly.

"Yup," Chloe replied. She went quiet for a minute, but it couldn't last. She slapped her knee and cracked up. "You guys are so funny. I know you want to hear all the news of what she was doing this morning, what she's wearing, the cute little things she said....She asked me to report back on you. What should I say?

"Tell her I'm looking smolderingly hot, and I'm not sweating like a monkey in my coveralls because I'm afraid of her dad."

"You're asking me to lie to her?"

"Do what you have to."

"You know what? We should have a double date: you and Betsy, me and Arthur."

Karl would love that. Being around Arthur made him a little anxious, only because he and George were identical twins who were really hard to tell apart, but maybe it would be like exposure therapy. "I'd love that. And yes, I was snooping for details."

"Aren't you two getting together tonight?"

"We were supposed to, but I'm not sure how late I'll be with your dad. I'll have to call her during lunch."

"I can tell her. I'm heading straight back after this."

"Hey, thanks."

"And Karl? I'm not trying to be all sappy or anything, but I'm really happy you two are together. Like, thrilled happy. As a sister, it was really tough to see Betsy not going for the good things that I knew she could have if she believed she was worthy of them. I was remembering back to last fall, when you told me she was getting into trouble at the bar, and something stood out to me."

Karl remembered too. Betsy had been dancing on Ed's pool table. Ed wasn't impressed. "What's that?"

"You were worried about her, but you said something about her just being a little lost, and that she'd find her way back. You were still rooting for her. That was a good example for me, because our sister Hannah and I, we made her feel like she was a screw-up sometimes, and you never did that. You saw the good in her."

Karl appreciated the compliment, but he didn't feel like he'd done anything special. "Happy I could help," he said. "You saw the evidence I delivered, so you know why I think she's pretty special." There it was. The wobbly voice.

"Okay. Too sappy now." Chloe said, getting up from her chair. "I'll tell Betsy you'll be a little late," she assured him. "Her crabby task master of a boss, is making her stay late, too. You two will be able to commiserate."

"Betsy's told me about her. She sounds like a better sister than she gives herself credit for."

"I *said* too sappy now." Chloe hopped into her truck.

She drove away, leaving Karl behind with his backlog of troubled vehicles and his racing thoughts.

Fortunately for Karl, he was presented with a couple of tricky problems later in the day that forced him to focus on his work. He figured both cars out by the end of the day, just in time to hand them back to their owners.

"You out there?" Frank called. Karl jumped so high he almost sailed over the back of the truck he was getting ready to start on.

He jumped a couple more times in an attempt to make it look like he was limbering up after a day of strenuous work rather than wound so tightly he was ready to snap. Frank obviously knew what Karl was up to. He cracked a smile.

"You wanna come into the office?"

"Yeah. Sure. Of course. I'll be right in." This job was scheduled for tomorrow anyway. He'd finish it up first thing in the morning. He ran his hands through his hair, making it look exactly the same as it always did, took a deep breath, and opened the office door.

"Surprise!"

Everyone was there: his mom, his dad, Nick, Betsy, Chloe, Arthur, Tammi, and of course, Frank. Streamers crisscrossed the ceiling and familiar balloons-leftovers from the fair perhaps-dangled from strings. A banner declaring *Congratulations Karl* stretched across the entrance.

Tammi ran outside and returned carrying an angel food cake topped with candles. As Betsy lit them, they all sang *For He's a Jolly Good Fellow* at the tops of their lungs, nobody louder than Karl's dad.

Blowing out the candles, Karl asked, "What's this all about?"

"It's about you buying the shop," his dad said, his face shining with pride and happiness.

"Looks like we're both going on new adventures." Nick slapped him on the back.

"I told everybody, and Tammi here insisted on throwing a surprise party," Frank said, putting his arm around his wife in a rare display of affection. "It turns out she's looking forward to having me around more often."

"You act so surprised, but you know I can't get enough of you." Tammi pinched Frank's cheek, and he pretended to be annoyed.

Betsy stood next to her parents, beaming. "Congratulations. It's your lucky day." She wrapped her arms around his neck and kissed him.

"My lucky day was yesterday," he whispered in her ear. "Today's a bonus."

Chapter Twenty-Five

In Which the Wedding Day Arrives at Last

"I can't believe you've been here a year," said Hugh, stretching his legs out in front of him and resting his feet on the ring of stones around the campfire. He took a swig of his beer and smacked his lips appreciatively. "Seriously. The local beer is so good."

Wes couldn't believe he'd been here that long either. When he'd arrived, the plan was to spend the summer at the pond, save the library, and leave without ever looking back. He'd been excited to spend more time with his mom, but he'd dreaded the prospect of seeing everyone else again, going so far as to hide behind a cardboard ice cream cone at Martel's to avoid being spotted by Bea.

She'd laughed when he told her about that. "What did you think I was going to do?"

He didn't know how to answer that. From the looks of her, she'd hardly changed since high school. She still had that long sheet of smooth brown hair and wore her pretty barn boots beneath a flowing ankle length skirt with lace at the hem. He supposed, when he thought about it now, that he was terrified that that beautiful farm girl would take one look at him and reject him all over again.

That's not what happened, though.

He'd never forget the first time they saw each other after all those years. They were both at a loss for words. It was as if a bolt of energy had coursed through them the moment their eyes met, erasing the time they'd spend apart and whatever had been holding them back from being together.

"Scott and I should move up here," Hugh continued. "We could set up a microbrewery of our own."

Wes would love it if Hugh lived here. They'd kept in touch a bit over the past year, but Hugh didn't have a cell phone or a computer. He wasn't the easiest guy to get a hold of.

On the other hand, the pace of life in Namur was slower than what Hugh was used to. It wasn't all summer parties, bonfires, and swimming in the pond. "I bet you guys would love it, but you might want to visit in the winter first. It gets really quiet then."

"Huh. Quiet could be alright. I'm starting to become more sedate in my later years," Hugh said formally.

"I don't believe you."

"For real. I'm thinking of settling down."

"Really?" Wes asked. "You mean you're thinking about getting married?"

"Thinking about it. Yeah."

"Do I get to be your best man?" Wes asked. He looked out over the dark pond. The stars twinkled overhead. In the light of the moon, two bats swooped out of the cedars on one side of the pond then disappeared on the other.

"You better be. You've held me back from doing so much stupid stuff. If you give me the Wes go-ahead, I'll know I'm making the right choice."

"I can already tell you that you are." Both Scott and Hugh were mechanics who liked to work on old cars, but Scott was another down to earth counterpoint to Hugh's lofty antics. They made a nice couple.

"Hey, do you want to take a swim?" Hugh didn't wait for a response, He kicked off his shoes, ran across the grassy path that wound around the length of the pond, barreled along the metal bridge that spanned it, and jumped in with a splash. Wes didn't want to go. He was warm by the fire, and the cool of the night prickled against his back.

Then again, when would he have another chance to do this? He'd be moving out tomorrow. Everything he owned was packed up in boxes and ready to go. It was mostly books. Bea had assured him that he could put up as many bookshelves as he wanted when he moved into the farmhouse. Did she fully understand what she'd agreed to?

Likely not.

Following the path that Hugh had taken, Wes launched off the bridge then collided with the smooth surface of the pond. Its heavy darkness pressed against him as he pulled his way up and took a deep breath of night air. Hugh whooped, splashed him, then flipped on his back and floated away towards the crackling fire.

"Wedding tomorrow," he called.

****

Wes's wedding day flew by in a series of moments. Hugh and Wes donning their tuxes in the morning, up way too early on account of Hugh waking Wes up to the soothing strains of *Jump Around.* Arriving at Saint Mary of the Snows, the church where Bea's parents, grandparents and great-grandparents and great-great-grandparents had been married before them. Standing at the front of the church with Hugh, Arthur, and Bea's brother Harvey. Looking out at the assembled crowd and realizing with a swell of gratitude how many of them had let him into their lives, had become like family. Chloe, Lindsay, Betsy, Grace, and Sarah walking down the aisle in soft yellow dresses, holding bouquets of the creamy white peonies that grew along the foundation of the farmhouse. Bea's niece Maddie, flinging petals down the aisle.

Then there was Bea...time stood still.

Their eyes met. She smiled. Wes smiled back. Her dad walked proudly beside her. Wes's mom and Claudette, seated next to each other in the front pew, dabbed at their eyes.

Time resumed its steady pace. Bea standing before him. Exchanging vows. Rings on fingers. Husband and wife. The kiss. Gliding back down the aisle. Driving to Cherry Bounce Inn. Alone for the first time together as husband and wife.

"What just happened?" Wes asked.

"I think we got married."

"We do have these rings on our fingers now." Wes held his up to the late afternoon sunlight that streamed in through the van's window.

"This has been the most perfect day...you look really tired. Did Hugh wake you up? I told him not to."

Wes laughed. "He might have."

"Do you think you'll make it to the end of the party?"

"I'll make it well past the end of the party." Wes gave Bea what he hoped was a wickedly sexy look.

"Do you have a bug in your eye?" Bea asked.

"Ha ha. Very funny. Yes, I do."

"I can't wait for every part of tonight," Bea said, running her hand along his arm then twining her fingers with his. How long would it take to sink in? He'd just married the only woman he'd ever loved, and he'd had the privilege of falling for her not once but twice.

"I can't wait either," he said.

They took the scenic route to Cherry Bounce Inn. By the time they got there, most of their guests had already arrived. The barn looked beautiful. Grace and Lindsay had worked their magic once again. All signs of the circus theme had been erased, replaced by white fairy lights, gauzy tulle, and sprays of white, light pink, and yellow flowers. Baby blue goblets crowded every table, awaiting a splash of effervescent champagne. At the head table long white tapered candles flickered from atop empty growlers of cider.

As they stood there admiring the scene, Bea and Wes were mobbed by a sea of yellow bridesmaids. “Congratulations you guys!” Chloe hugged Bea so tightly she nearly lifted her off the ground.

Bea smoothed her dress and caught her breath. “Thanks. Now that I’m married, I have a sneaking suspicion the rest of you won’t be far behind. You went along with my crazy Demeter Society plan, so I’m thinking you’ll follow me anywhere.”

“None of your plans are crazy, but I can’t believe you two are married. It’s only taken you twenty years to get here,” said Chloe.

“And it might never have happened if it wasn’t for Sarah,” Wes chimed in.

“Me?” Sarah looked shocked at the suggestion that she had been the one to bring the two lovebirds together.

“Absolutely,” said Wes. “You were the one who came into the old library and told me that Bea still had feelings for me. I worried it was too good to be true, but apparently it wasn’t, because it all worked out. You gave us the nudge we needed to get back together.”

“Oh, well, I’d be pleased to take a little credit. You do know how I love a good romance. I’ll have to get working on some of the other couples around here.”

“Me next!” said Chloe and Lindsay at the same time.

They laughed, but Chloe didn’t look like she was fully joking when she turned to Bea and stage whispered, “Aim for me when you throw the bouquet.”

Bea nodded seriously, and Wes couldn't help but feel sorry for her as Betsy, Grace, and Lindsay gasped.

"You can't aim for anyone specific," Lindsay insisted. "That's favoritism. Besides, if anyone should be favored, it should be the person who's dating your brother. Harvey's your only sibling, and he's being so kind as to tend to the farm tomorrow morning with his kids while you sleep in at a beautiful all-inclusive historic bed and breakfast."

Wes happened to know that Lindsay didn't need the extra dose of luck that the bouquet was rumored to provide. Harvey had already bought a ring and was waiting for the right moment to propose, but he wouldn't dream of ruining the surprise.

"You guys do realize it isn't necessarily true that the first person to catch the bouquet will be the next one to get married, right? It's just a superstition," said Bea. Lindsay and Chloe shrugged, apparently unconvinced. "Besides, maybe you can have a double wedding," she added.

"Oooh. She's right," said Chloe. "Or a quadruple one."

Betsy gasped.

"I was only kidding."

"It's not that," Betsy said, leaning forward a bit and wincing. "I've been having really strong contractions all day. I thought they were practice ones, because they were really far apart, but they're coming much closer together now."

Chloe was by her side in an instant with her

hand on her back, her face full of concern. "What do you want me to do?"

"Can you find Karl? I think he's sitting over there with his parents." Betsy motioned to the other side of the barn, which was obscured by a crowd of people, milling about and chatting. Chloe nodded and sprinted away.

"Our anniversary and your baby's birthday might end up being the same day," said Bea.

"I'm not ready." Betsy closed her eyes and breathed deeply. "She doesn't have a name yet."

Wes smiled, recalling how inspired he was when the goats were born. It was easier to choose their names once he could see them in person. He wasn't sure if Betsy would appreciate the analogy, however. "It'll come to you," was all he said.

Chloe returned with Karl and Tammi.

"Is it time?" Tammi asked. Betsy nodded. "Are you sure? You're a little early."

Betsy took a long shuddering breath. "I'm sure."

"Oh my goodness. My first grandchild. Hannah's late; you're early. I can't believe it."

Karl pulled Betsy into a hug and whispered something in her ear. Her face relaxed as she leaned into him. All of the women hugged Betsy and wished her luck then Karl and Tammi walked her out the door.

Wow. A baby and a wedding. This was a big day. Wes scanned the room. Most of their guests hadn't noticed the excitement by the front door. Wes's mom and his Uncle Stephen sat together at another table, both with a plate of hors d'oeuvres.

Bea squeezed Wes's hand then wandered off to talk with a group of her cousins. They were already laughing, probably reminiscing about their grandparents, who had been very much loved and very much characters.

And speaking of characters, Roy sat at a nearby table, regaling Patrick with a loud story about one of his many personal successes. "How ya doin'?" Roy boomed when Wes sat down to join them. "I was just telling Pat here that Sarah and I have gotten into walking together. She calls it 'power walking', but it seems to me it's just swinging your arms and walking fast. I call that plain old walking. Sorry I got a little testy with you the other day." Roy thumped Wes on the back. It smarted. Wes should've seen that coming and given Roy a wider berth. "I owe you one, now that you've got us on this health kick. My doctor will be thanking you too...Hey, I bet I'll be able to out-walk *you* pretty soon, young librarian."

Wes mumbled something between a yeah and a no. It came out as a neah. Getting into a competition with Roy was nearly as fraught with danger as denying Roy the chance to compete.

"Anyway," Roy went on. "Maybe you know a thing or two about a thing or two. Might catch up with me one day if you keep working at it." He got up, chuckling. "I'm going to make the rounds. Gotta shake hands when you're a local celebrity."

When Roy had gone, Patrick and Wes were left

alone at the table. "What a lovely day," said Patrick. "You'll have a happy life together. I can tell. Your wife looks at you the way mine looked at me, and I consider myself one of the luckiest men I know when it comes to love."

Bea, who was still mingling with their guests, caught Wes's eye from across the room. Her eyes went soft. She smiled.

"I feel the same way," Wes said. "Like this is the beginning of something that took root a long time ago."

Chapter Twenty-Six

In Which Love Finds a Way

Betsy's heart was full to overflowing as she cradled her newborn baby in her arms. Bernadette Rose smelled of softness and warm milk and something else that Betsy couldn't quite pinpoint but felt familiar somehow, like a sweet memory she'd forgotten from childhood.

Bernadette's squishy red face was pressed to Betsy's breast as she nursed. Tiny wrinkled fingers and rough little fingernails prickled and scratched at Betsy's skin. Betsy folded the flaps of fabric on the end of Bernadette's sleeves to protect her precious face from those pointy nails while Karl adjusted her tiny striped hat.

"Can you believe it?" he asked. "You did that. You made her and got her out into the world. You're amazing."

Betsy couldn't believe it. When would it truly sink in that she would be going home with this precious little girl? Whatever Betsy had done or hadn't done in the past faded away when she looked ahead to a future with her baby and the man sitting beside them.

"Thank you for being here with me. This doesn't seem real, does it? I mean, look at her."

Karl did. "She's adorable. Her eyebrows are doing that scrunchy thing that yours do when you're worried."

Betsy considered. "She does look concerned right now, like she's really pondering this new development in her life."

"Two thoughtful women...I can come back home with you to stay for a while, if you want me to," Karl said, smoothing Betsy's hair off her forehead. "I know you can handle it, but you might get a bit more sleep with someone there to help you, to take care of you two."

"The fact that you're offering means so much to me, but my mom will be staying at my house for a few nights when I get back."

"Oh, sure. Of course." Karl shifted in his seat. "I don't want to bug you at all. Just know that I'm here, and you can ask me for anything, anytime."

Betsy did know that, and she was incredibly tempted to tell him to move right in. "To be honest, I'd love to have you at my house all the time, for all kinds of reasons."

"Me too..."

"But then I think about everything that's happened between us, and it seems like it would be better to slow things down. We have so much time to be together now. I don't want to rush because of the baby or because we already know each other so well...I hope that makes sense."

"You're right. It would be so easy and comfortable to jump in like we're an old couple. I want to be with you two all the time, but we should date a while and figure everything out."

"Exactly. Thank you for understanding. I would never want you to feel like I'm pushing you away."

"No. You're right. I get it. I'm just struggling to resist your charms."

Betsy's nipples were sore, her stomach was crampy, her hair was greasy and tangled, and there was Karl, looking at her like she was the most beautiful woman he'd ever seen. Bernadette squeaked. She'd slipped off Betsy's breast and fallen asleep. Betsy snuggled her close. "Do you want to hold her?"

"I'd love to. Why don't I dim the lights? You can nap. It's two o'clock already."

"What?" Betsy looked at the clock. She hadn't realized it had gotten so late.

Karl stood up and turned the lights down. The instant he did, Betsy's eyes and limbs felt heavy and warm. Karl brushed his lips against hers, feather soft. He kissed Bernadette on her cap. Betsy shifted her baby in her arms and handed her off to Karl. Pulling his chair closer to her, Karl sat back down and nudged Bernadette's pink receiving blanket away from her barely there chin to better see her face.

Betsy, turning on her side to face the two people she loved most in the world, snuggled into her pillow and closed her eyes. She drifted off into a heavy dreamless sleep.

Chapter Twenty-Seven

In Which Karl Takes a Stand

"What are you doing here?"

Karl turned around. He'd been coming back up from the cafeteria, where he'd grabbed a cup of fruit and a bagel, when a voice from behind him stopped him in his tracks. It was George. Betsy had asked Chloe to call him whenever she went into labor, but she'd told Karl that she wasn't sure if or when he'd show up. They had their answer. He was showing up at noon the day after his daughter was born.

Karl took a steadying breath, determined to maintain his composure in the face of the man who had threatened to expose him. When he was as ready as he was going to be, he turned around. "Hi."

"You heard me." George was headed his way. "What are you doing here?" Karl was taken aback by the hostility in George's voice.

"I'm here to support Betsy," he replied, trying to mask his own anger. "We're dating, and she's my oldest friend. Congratulations on the birth of your daughter. She's beautiful."

George strode up to him until their noses were practically touching. "I know you went to Tom, but it doesn't change anything between us. Who do you think you are? You can't blackmail me. I don't want you anywhere near Betsy or Bernadette."

"Well, that's not really up to you," Karl said. He backed up a step. George, the master of bland arrogance, looked as though steam could've shot out his ears. Karl almost pitied him. George had always, always gotten his way, and he didn't know what to do when he couldn't do whatever he wanted while everyone else fell in line.

Choosing his words carefully, not wanting to make anything worse for Betsy but unwilling to back down, Karl said, "I'm completely uninterested in getting into a competition with you. I won't do it. You've chosen not to be with Betsy, and she has chosen to be with me. That's it. That's all there is to it."

George started to interrupt, but Karl held up his hand and talked over him, attracting some stares from patients in a nearby waiting room. "You have a beautiful daughter. I suggest you go upstairs and meet her, and when you do, think about what's best for her and what's best for Betsy. I assure you, that's what I'm doing and will continue to do. If you ever consider having this conversation with me again, remember what I just said. It should cover any other questions you might have."

George huffed and stomped away.

Karl took a circuitous route back to Betsy's room and sat down in an uncomfortable plastic chair in a deserted hallway to eat his lunch. Tammi had come back to the hospital that morning and was in the room with Betsy for the time being.

After Karl had eaten his last grape, he took his time walking back to Betsy's room. When he finally got there and peeked inside, George was sitting by the bed, holding Bernadette with a look of tender wonder on his face. He didn't say anything when Karl walked into the room, but he did give him a begrudging nod. Karl nodded back. It was a start.

"I wanted to check on you, but I'll leave you guys for a little bit." Karl gave a small wave to Tammi, slipped Betsy a bag of her favorite kettle chips, then stepped back out of the room.

He went outside and took a couple of laps around the hospital. The scent of freshly mown grass, warmed by the strong summer sun, was a welcome change from the chemical smell of the hospital. On his third lap, Karl came across George, climbing into his flashy sports car. He had probably seen Karl as well, but he didn't acknowledge him as he raced out of the lot.

Back inside, Betsy was alone with Bernadette, nursing her and smoothing her little forehead. She looked up when Karl came into the room.

She shook her head in disbelief, "You," she said. "You're incredible. Where have you been all my life?"

"Here," he said, making his way to her side. "I've been right here all along."

Chapter Twenty-Eight

In Which Wes Carries On

Wes pulled the Door County Bookmobile into the parking lot of Saint Mary of the Snows Catholic Church. The unfurled maple leaves cast a cool shadow over his favorite spot, and the church doors were propped open, permitting a warm summer breeze to make its way inside the church. He scanned the perimeter, spying a single patron. Tom waited for him in the grassy lawn. Wes put the bus in park and unlocked the door. Tom climbed inside. He strolled the length of the stacks. He tipped a couple of books, inspecting their titles then replacing them without another glance. He sat down. He sighed.

"What's up?" Wes asked, spinning around in his seat.

"Oh boy. Wait until you hear this one..." Tom began.

The End

Author's Note

Although the people and many of the specific places in this tale come entirely from my imagination, Namur, Wisconsin is a real town and a little known National Historic Landmark in Southern Door County. It is nestled at the base of a peninsula that separates the waters of Green Bay and Lake Michigan. In the mid-1800s, Belgian immigrant families from the French speaking region of Wallonia settled the area, and it remains one of the longest-standing immigrant enclaves in the United States. The red brick farmhouses, roadside chapels, and summer kitchens still dot the landscape, and the local delicacies are on display every year at the Kermiss harvest festival.

My favorite part of writing, other than getting to spend time with my characters, is hearing from readers. Please consider leaving a review of Cedar Hollow Summer on Amazon. All feedback is appreciated, as it helps me grow as a writer and will help direct others to a series that they may enjoy as well. Thank you so very much.

What's Next?

The Happy Endings Apothecary by author Amanda Schwantes. Coming January 2021.

The Happy Endings Apothecary of Pine Mountain, Wisconsin is a bookstore for patrons who are serious about their happily ever afters. It also served as a haven for brothers Blake and Griffin, who spent much of their troubled childhood amongst its magical stacks. Now all grown up and working as wildland firefighters, a tragic accident sends the brothers back to their hometown. As Blake struggles to recover from his injuries with the help of Stephanie, his childhood best friend, their growing closeness prompts both Stephanie and Blake to face the past and make big decisions about their futures. Along the way they're helped by a young banjoist, a lonely cat, and a book club of women who are sometimes badly behaved and always there for their friends.

www.ingramcontent.com/pod-product-compliance
Lightning Source LLC
LaVergne TN
LVHW091038080826
845145LV00002B/539

* 9 7 8 1 7 3 5 7 5 0 8 2 8 *